SHADOW RUN

A.C. JETT

Questions/comments? The author can be contacted at AuthorACJett@gmail.com.

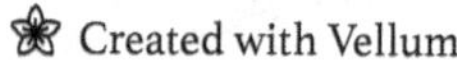 Created with Vellum

1

"A*ny sufficiently advanced technology is indistinguishable from magic.*"
- Arthur C. Clarke

In a motel room, bathed in the dim glow of a low-wattage bulb, the wind whistled through the torn valance. It brought a dusting of snow that filtered into the room, settling atop a precarious tower of old newspapers. Huddled in bed, Jack Bradford, who had seen better years, wrote with manic energy. He ripped out page after page from his pad, each discarded idea ending up as another crumpled paper ball on the floor around him. An open bottle of Scotch was within arm's reach, but it brought him little comfort. Solitary, with only his thoughts and the words on his pages for company.

A pile of photographs caught his attention, and he began thumbing through them. One, in particular, caught his eye: a black-and-white image of strangers waving at him from inside the hold of an airplane. It was clear from the picture that Jack had once been a man of great charm. Unnoticed, the soft tap-tap-tap of someone typing filled the room.

Suddenly the roar of an airplane's engines filled his ears, and he stood amongst parachutists, wearing nothing but blue striped pajamas. He grinned and waved at the photographer, then, without hesitation, he jumped without a parachute.

Jack woke with a start, the dampness of cold sweat soaking through his pajamas. He reached out instinctively, but the bed beside him was cold and empty. The lingering signs of a woman's presence filled the room: the scent of perfume, jewelry on the nightstand, and delicate lingerie peeping out from an open chest. Even a walk-in closet filled with clothes. The portrait of a stunning woman dominated one wall, her face obscured by shadows. A strip of black velvet was clipped to one corner of the frame.

"Beth?" Jack called out into the quiet night, but only silence replied. "Beth," he repeated, a note of desperation creeping into his voice.

The scene shifted again, revealing a living room, a picture of neglect and decay. Evidence of a solitary existence littered the room: liquor bottles, fast food wrappers, unemptied ashtrays, and wilting plants.

Sinking onto the couch with a hefty pour of Scotch, Jack lit a cigarette. His sheepdog, Athena, leaped onto his chest, her tongue lapping at his face.

"No, Athena. Come on," he protested half-heartedly, but the dog was undeterred. "You want something to eat? Mom doesn't feed you anymore, does she?"

He refilled his glass, which Athena sniffed at curiously. "No, you don't want this, only for daddy, girl. We'll get you something soon. -- Mom's not coming back, you know."

He downed his Scotch in one gulp, his eyes welling up from

the smoke. An orange and black mass caught his attention in the corner – a parachutist's jump gear, a memento of a past life, a past self.

A Few Days Earlier

As dawn broke over the airfield, the chill in the air was palpable, the sort of cold that crystallized breath and made your skin tingle. A crew had already assembled; radio personnel from KLOQ, jump staff from Parachutes Inc., and a hodgepodge of eager spectators gathered around a massive butterfly tent.

Without warning, Jack emerged, now clean-shaven and clad in a shiny black and orange jumpsuit. The crowd erupted into cheers as a small band struck up a lively tune. Hands clapped him on the back, offering congratulations and encouragement.

"Here's morning's Number One man, Jack Bradford," an announcer proclaimed over the din.

A professionally dressed woman, Jack's producer, beamed at him. "How was ground school, Bradford?" she inquired.

"Piece of cake," he replied nonchalantly.

He found his hand being vigorously shaken by a frumpy chairwoman. "You don't know how grateful we are for you doing this, Mr. Bradford. On behalf of Children's Hospital, I can't thank you enough."

He offered a gracious smile. "A pleasure to help out."

A female reporter entered the conversation, running her hand along Jack's smooth chin. "Mmm, I'm sure it is. You getting a little nervous, Jackie boy?" she asked teasingly.

Jack extended his arm, holding it steady as a rock. "Never. Nerves of steel."

Yet, his wide-eyed expression told a different story. Undeterred, he continued his journey through the crowd, exchanging handshakes and pleasantries. The reporter turned back to the announcer once he had moved on, a knowing look in her eyes. "He's nervous alright."

"From twelve thousand feet? Who wouldn't be?" the announcer concurred with a chuckle.

As Jack neared the plane, an engineer secured a portable radio transmitter onto his chest. "I've rigged it so the mic will always be on. You just keep talking, and we'll pick you up."

"All the pieces? Promise?" Jack asked, his tone demanding reassurance.

"Yeah, sure," the engineer replied dismissively.

But Jack persisted. "Seriously. How am I supposed to take my call-ins?"

Meanwhile, a jump instructor had started fastening a buckle on Jack's shoulder. "How's that? Tight enough?"

"Make it any tighter my right arm will fall off," Jack quipped.

"Wouldn't want to do that. You got to pull with your right," the instructor advised him.

"What if I'm left-handed?" Jack asked a mischievous glint in his eyes.

2

———

The throng of well-wishers ushered Jack up the steps of the DC3, their voices a cacophony of cheers and words of encouragement. At the fringe of the crowd, the producer and the engineer shared a moment of respite.

"Never quits trying to kill himself, does he?" the producer mused, watching Jack's back. "The man's certainly got guts."

"That's not what I call it," the engineer retorted an undercurrent of disapproval in his tone.

Suddenly, the reporter burst through the mass of bodies, rushing up the steps to Jack. She brandished a microphone like a weapon, inserting it into his personal space. "Before we take off, Bradford. One final question."

"And one final answer," he responded, his tone casual.

"We're on the air, Bradford."

"I hope so. I always answer questions when I'm on the air. What I can't figure out, though, is how I'm supposed to take those phone calls."

"You won't need to."

"Why? Did they cancel my show?" Jack's words were playful, the humor evident in his voice.

The reporter's demeanor shifted, becoming strictly professional. "Several listeners have called this morning and want to know if you're worried about drifting off course, landing in the water, that sort of thing. Doesn't that scare you?"

"Why should it? I can swim." Jack's response was bold, eliciting applause from the crowd. He grinned at his instructor, raised a hand to wave at his fans, and stepped inside the plane. His support team filed in after him.

The producer cast a sideways glance at the engineer, her expression contemplative. "Too glib. More than usual. Think he's been drinking?"

"Wouldn't blame him. He's been like that ever since he lost them," the engineer replied, his gaze fixed on the now-closed plane door. "Hides it well, though."

The DC3's propellers roared to life, sending a gust of wind hurtling down the runway. Checks were made, the navy and white plane picked up speed, and then it lifted, a mechanical bird taking to the sky.

Inside the cockpit, the pilot expertly leveled off at 12,000 feet, a sea of clouds obscuring the landscape below. "All set," the jump instructor said, his voice echoing in the cabin.

A sound man busied himself in the holding area with a final check of Jack's equipment. At the same time, the reporter ensured every second was captured on tape. A jump coach, dressed in pristine white coveralls, tightened his own harness before passing a helmet to Jack. A photographer snapped pictures nonstop, the flash creating miniature sunbursts in the cabin.

"Thirty seconds free fall. Then pull," the jump coach instructed, his voice brimming with authority.

"Ground requests keep it short and sweet, Bradford. No screaming, no swearing, she said. Or we cut you off," the sound-man warned, adjusting a few knobs on his soundboard.

"Ah shit," Jack grumbled, earning him a reproachful glance from the reporter.

"Jack, this is an incredible moment. Aren't you excited?" she asked, her voice a sugar-coated plea.

"I'm too excited for words, Bambi," he replied, his tone mocking.

"Remember to aim for the X, just like we talked about. Danny here'll guide you down, so don't sweat it," the jump instructor advised, gesturing to the jump coach.

"What if he hits me?" Jack asked, the question causing a round of stifled laughter.

"Never happen," the jump instructor replied with a shake of his head.

"I saw it in a film once. Guy got slammed. Landed five hundred miles away," Jack mused aloud, earning more chuckles.

"Bradford? Just one more," the photographer requested, aiming his camera.

Jack assumed the pose he had taken in the motel room, his face a mask of forced cheerfulness. The camera clicked, capturing a moment suspended in time.

The morning sky above the clouds was an expanse of brilliant blue. Its silence shattered as a DC3 came into view. The aircraft seemed to hang in the sky before a door slid open, revealing an orange figure - Jack Bradford. He paused momentarily, perhaps appreciating the serenity of the high altitude, then fearlessly plunged into the void. Seconds later, a white figure followed, the pair swallowed by the thick white sea of clouds.

They spiraled and spun, spread-eagled in the expansive sky,

their dive accompanied by the hiss of radio static and Jack's uneven breathing.

"Whew! Right on schedule. Bradford in the morning on KLOQ," Jack's voice crackled over the radio. "First couple of hundred feet really takes your breath away. Gotta count, though. Fifty-five, fifty-four..."

Inside the DC3, the crew clustered around a receiver, their faces a mixture of amusement and concern.

"What's he doing?" the reporter asked, her brows furrowed.

"Scared. Counting wrong. Happens all the time," the jump instructor explained, a smirk tugging at the corner of his lips.

"Very funny, Jack," the sound man chimed in, his voice a mix of amusement and anxiety.

On the airfield, Jack's producer squinted at the sky through binoculars, her heart pounding. Next to her, the announcer chain-smoked, his attention riveted on his remote booth.

"The weather's fine up here, folks. Traffic's good too. Like always. Thirty-seven, thirty-six, thirty-five, thirty-four," Jack's voice echoed over the radio.

Through her binoculars, the producer spotted Jack and the jump coach. The white parachute of the coach burst open, the KLOQ logo proudly displayed against the sky. But Jack, a dot of orange against the blue, was still in free fall, his parachute stubbornly shut.

"Pull the chute, Jack," the producer muttered, a sense of dread creeping into her voice.

"Thirty. Well, it's all downhill now, folks," Jack's voice filled the air, an eerie calm replacing the earlier apprehension. "This is Bradford in the morning on KLOQ radio signing off. What a finale! What a show!"

3

———————

On the airfield, the crowd stood in awe. The producer turned towards the engineer, her tone sharp.

"Cut him off? What is this? Some kind of joke? He's supposed to pull that thing," she said.

"I think he's having trouble," replied the engineer, concern evident in his voice.

"Get the emergency crew over here. I don't want a dead Bradford on my hands."

Meanwhile, Jack continued his descent in the sky, his voice crackling over the radio, "Fifteen, fourteen, thirteen. My lucky number. Hope it's yours."

"Shut him off," the producer commanded. The engineer hit a switch, silencing Jack. Suddenly, the announcer's voice filled the air.

"We seem to be experiencing some technical difficulty, but we'll be right back with Bradford's live jump right after this brief interlude on the big clock, KLOQ."

The chairwoman looked skyward, her hands clasped in prayer. "Sweet Jesus, he's going to die," she murmured.

. . .

In the sky, Jack passed into a low-lying cloud and disappeared. A splash of color followed the parachute, opening wide and slowly floating toward the ground. The crowd erupted in cheers, and the producer exhaled, relief washing over her.

"Thanks for the cardiac arrest, Jack," she muttered.

Moments later, a Jeep pulled up with the head of the jump team. "Let's bring him in," he said. They sped off towards the landing site.

Jack's parachute touched down in the center of a huge white 'X' painted on the grassy field. It collapsed on impact, but there was no sign of Jack.

"Bradford? Hey Bradford, you alright? Where are you?" the jump coach shouted, peering through the billowing silk of the parachute. The crew looked around, their faces mirroring their confusion.

"Anyone see him land?" asked the producer. But there was only silence and the rustling of the parachute in the wind. The harness was buckled and intact, but there was no sign of Jack.

"What happened? Where's Bradford?" the reporter asked.

"Haven't the faintest. A practical joke. A little magic. How's that?" replied the producer, though she was as confused as everyone else.

Suddenly, a voice burst out from across the field. A small boy raced towards them, shouting, "Dad, hey, dad. Back here. He's over here."

Turning towards the source of the voice, they rushed towards the main tent. Pushing through the crowd, they found Jack Bradford lying on the ground, a blanket being placed over him by paramedics. His face was covered in blood, his jumpsuit torn, and the transmitter was gone.

"Jack, you alright? Can you hear me? Jack?" the producer asked, her voice shaky.

Jack's eyes were unfocused, staring into space. When the producer asked him to say something, anything, all he managed to whisper were incomprehensible words. "Xyrak lysooda Fyrapo."

As the paramedics loaded Jack onto a stretcher and rushed him to an ambulance, the producer warned everyone, "What you see here does not leave this group. Understood?"

The crowd remained silent, dumbfounded by what they had just witnessed. As the ambulance drove away, the producer climbed in, leaving behind a cloud of dust and unanswered questions.

The ambulance roared past the anxious crowd, leaving a trail of dust in its wake as it disappeared into the distance. None of them knew the full story of what happened to Jack, at least not yet.

Inside the moving ambulance, the producer was jostled as the vehicle raced down the bumpy road. She wiped the blood from Jack's face, dismissing the paramedic hovering nearby. Noticing that Jack had difficulty breathing, she quickly placed an oxygen mask over his face. She waited for some sign of recognition to return to his blank, unseeing eyes. She touched the rugged beard that had sprouted seemingly out of nowhere in the span of ten minutes.

"Things'll be alright, Jack. I'll take care of you. Just trust me," she murmured, her voice barely audible over the sounds of the ambulance's sirens.

From Jack's perspective, the world was a blur. Trees whizzed past, freeway ramps flashed in and out of sight, and traffic sounds were faint under the ambulance's wailing siren. The partially clouded blue sky began to take shape in his vision.

"People don't just disappear for no reason," Jack mused, his voice echoing hollowly in his own mind. "But how could I tell them that? Took me years to realize that my entire life had been turned upside down in just five minutes. A hard slap in the face for pulling that suicide stunt."

His thoughts shifted, and he was suddenly back in the sky that morning, watching the DC3 float into view. The plane was graceful, seeming to blink in and out of existence as it navigated the clouds. Its side door slid open, revealing the dark, womb-like interior of the plane. The past and present mingled, a stark reminder of the surreal events of the day.

4

Inside the holding area of the DC3, the noise of the wind and engines was deafening. Shouts echoed around the cabin, mixed with the crew's chaotic flurry of hand signals. One last photo was taken a snapshot before Jack fearlessly dove out of the aircraft and into the open sky.

The view was breathtaking. Experiencing the thrill of freefalling firsthand, he could feel the soothing pull of Mother Earth tugging at his limbs, the wind buffeting against him, beckoning him closer. His heart pounded in his chest, adrenaline coursing through his veins.

"Forty-one, forty. The weather's fine up here, folks. Traffic's good too. Like always," Jack murmured, the ground racing up to meet him with alarming speed. He could see the details of the crowd, the wiper blades on the planes, and the dust settling on the tent.

A peaceful smile settled on Jack's face as he watched the coach's parachute flare open above him. He folded his arms over his chest and continued to plummet downward, speeding toward the ground faster and faster.

"This is Bradford in the morning on KLOQ radio signing

off," he said, a note of finality in his voice. No one knew when he pulled the rip cord or if he ever did. All Jack knew was the sudden, powerful force pulling him upward, wrenching at his arms, and the white clouds around him that began to envelop him.

Suddenly, he twisted in the landscape dissolved, transforming into a stark, snow-covered field at night. Jack was tumbling down a steep incline, thick ice blocks slamming against his flailing arms. He gathered speed, avalanching down the slope until it evened into a gentle swell. His snow-covered body finally came to rest, lifeless and still.

The wind whistled eerily, piercing the quiet night with an Arctic shrill. After a moment of silence, a strained cough broke the stillness. A freezing finger poked through the snow, laboriously digging its way out. Soon, a head followed, and Jack emerged from the snow, peering around through pained eyes at his unfamiliar surroundings.

5

T he snowfield rose dramatically, leading to the start of a majestic peak hidden behind a dense layer of maroon-colored clouds. The eerie greenish glow of the snow around him hinted that night had fallen.

"Where am I? Snow? What's snow doing here?" Jack murmured, puzzled.

Looking around, the bright green hues made him squint to discern shapes nearby. It almost looked like night vision without the goggles.

"Geez, this is death? I could have gone to Alaska if I'd known it would be like this," he joked, attempting to lighten his heavy mood.

Rising to his feet, Jack found himself lacking his usual balance. He staggered around in a tight circle, focused on the strange sky above him.

"No, seriously folks, this isn't death. This is just a hallucination. I'm probably in the hospital right now, and they're operating on me. All the king's horses and all the king's men couldn't put old Jack together again," he mused aloud, his voice echoing off the silent landscape.

But his words were cut off as he tripped, tumbling down the slope. A sharp pain shot through his shoulder, causing him to wince.

"Alright, Jack, let's just think this one through," he reassured himself, surveying the landscape again. One way led up to the maroon clouds, while the other directed toward a few distant trees where the snow gradually ceased.

"It's night. I jumped at eight in the morning, and now it's night. Okay no problem. So I was knocked out, and they flew me to Greenland. Got a little delirious, left the hospital, and now I'm wandering around in the snow. Simple," he reasoned, standing up with some difficulty.

His gaze hardened, focusing on the horizon. Beyond the trees, the sky seemed to lighten. "Looks like Northern lights or something," he speculated.

Dropping down on one knee, Jack steadied his gaze, watching the horizon. "No change. Weird," he muttered.

Suddenly, he stood and shouted at the top of his lungs, "Where's the hospital? Anybody there?"

"There, there, there." His words echoed in the far canyon, a desperate repetition. In a frantic pitch, he screamed, "Help!" The word hung in the air, ringing in the silent, snowy landscape.

"Help, elp, elp, elp," the echo of Jack's distressed cry bounced back to him. Unhinged by fear and uncertainty, he began to run, stumbling and turning, always on the brink of tumbling down the frozen slope.

"Somebody. Anyone. Answer me. Where am I?" he called out into the seemingly unending expanse of snow.

The wind responded, whipping up eddies of snow, and traces of ground lightning whizzed past, sporadic and far off.

"Help me. This isn't fair. What's happening to me? Where'd everyone go?" The wind snatched his words away, only the echo reverberating, "Go, go, go." Blinded, he stumbled and fell face-first into a drift.

Upon opening his eyes, he was greeted with nothing but the shrill whine of the wind above his head, constant and uninterrupted. The world was devoid of any other sound. Sitting up, he wiped the snow from his face and murmured, "Fuck it. There's got to be a McDonald's around here someplace."

Adrenaline propelled him to his feet, and he began to race down the mountain again.

"Sure, the sky's the wrong color, and the moon doesn't move, but so what? You can't fool Bradford In The Morning," he declared, his words slicing through the silent night.

His pace quickened. "I owe you one, Janice. Boy, do I owe you? This prank is your doing. I know it. And you're still listening to me, aren't you?" His hand slapped against the transmitter on his chest, checking it. A red recording light blinked back at him. It was still on.

"Well, you can all come in and get me now. Nice bit while it worked. Probably picked up your lousy ratings. But you can't fool Jack Brad..."

Without warning, the mountain fell away beneath him. An avalanche. He found himself flung through the maroon-tinted night, the echo of his name hauntingly bouncing back at him.

With a harsh slam, he crashed into a cluster of dead trees, frozen and fragile as ice. Jack's body collided with the trunk hitting him in the backside and sending him upside down. A deep, aching groan ripped from his throat.

His world flipped upside down. Snow appeared to fall upwards. Small tornado-like eddies spiraled around him, yellow flashes flaring up and vanishing as quickly as they appeared, leaving only a thin stream of snow in their wake. In the maroon glow of the sky, twin moons spun silently above him in a rapid orbit. Stunned and silent, Jack rolled onto his knees, his mind struggling to comprehend his surreal surroundings.

6

An endless expanse of zinc-green white stretched out in every direction, punctuated by gnarled, dead trees, their skeletal forms pointing accusingly at the sky. Jack moved cautiously down the mountain, supporting himself with a branch, every step tested before being trusted.

"I don't know if anyone's listening," he began, his voice bouncing between courage, apprehension, and despair. "But I've spent fifteen years talking to myself, never knowing if anyone was out there. If anyone wants to call, I could sure use a friendly voice."

As he surveyed the foreign surroundings, his speech became progressively slurred, the freezing temperature finally taking its toll, adding a shiver to his voice.

"First, I thought I was dead, but then I don't suppose you shiver like this in heaven. Maybe you didn't make it that far, Bradford. Great."

Alone on the windswept slope, he talked to the microphone and transmitter strapped to his chest, his voice echoing back in his ears.

"Funny how radio people talk about themselves in the third

person. Hey Bradford? -- Yeah. -- Get that guy off this hill. -- We're working on it. -- I hope so."

Above him, behind the maroon cloud cover, two spheres of reflected light continued their eternal dance, tracing arcs from one horizon to the next. Jack stood still, awestruck by the spectacle.

"I don't know what time it is on the big clock. Don't know what morning traffic's like either. But KLOQ's Bradford can tell you the big news of the day -- I'm not on earth."

7

He faced a narrow, icy passage tinted in a strange greenish hue. Warm steam billowed from scattered ice caves, the diamond-patterned walls appearing solid. A cramped opening forced him to stoop and half-crawl through the descending pathway.

"Oh, give me a home where the buffalo roam and the deer and the antelope play..." he sang, his voice bouncing off the icy walls, a vain attempt to keep his spirits high and his sanity intact.

He squeezed his bulky, orange-clad figure through a bluish ice pipe, then smashed through a thin crystal wall. He landed in another greenish area, his progress hindered by a collection of stalactites as he inched further along the icy corridor.

"... where seldom is heard, a discouraging word and the skies are not cloudy all day -- ay -- ay." He tried to protect his hands from the biting frost by using the frozen walls for support.

A slip, a slide, and he was hurtling like a lightning bolt down a sixty-foot bobsled run. When he reached the bottom, he picked himself up, pain radiating from various parts of his body.

A dark silhouette in the shape of a man stared back at him

from inside a steam-filled, fluorescent cave. The figure was nothing more than a shadow.

Jack felt a strange sensation, his gaze drawn upwards, uncertain of what his eyes relayed.

"Hello? Who's there? Who are you?" His voice bounced around him, echoing back unanswered. The shadow he'd seen was eerily static, seeming to wax and wane in his vision.

"Hello?" He tried again, but the unease grew. He blinked, and when his eyes found the spot again, the shadow disappeared. "Terrific. Now I'm seeing things."

With a grunt, he picked himself up, tested one leg, then limped past a snow block and deeper into the icy interior.

Inside the mist-filled emerald cavern, not one nor two, but a half-dozen Shadows congregated. They appeared to study one another, exchanging soft, alien sounds. As each one responded and turned sideways, they vanished from sight as if by magic.

He stood at the edge of a sweeping, boulder-strewn canyon. Steaming water cascaded from one level to another, collecting in deep jade and cyan pools below. Jack picked his way down the rugged slope, pausing to take in the strange sight under the maroon sky.

He hummed, "*I left my heart in San Francisco. Hmm, hmm, mmm hmm, above the bay.*" He sang quietly to himself, tinkering with the transmitter strapped to his chest, snapping his fingers to a slow tap rhythm. He snapped a piece of ice off the device, returning it to working condition.

"*People always talk about what scares them. Big snakes, heights, the dark. I figure we're all afraid of one thing -- being alone.*" Jack mused to himself, rubbing his hands and blowing on them to stave off the numbing cold, to keep the blood flowing.

"*I wasn't on earth anymore. Hadn't any idea where I was, how I got here, or why. I also knew I'd never see home again. Tough to imagine being more alone than that."*

His eyes swept across the stretch of the canyon in all its majesty. A grouping of slender trees stretched towards the cloud-infested sky, their long shadows casting a stark chiaroscuro across the harsh landscape. With a determined look, Jack began his descent into the bowels of the canyon.

"Had to keep myself going. Downhill was easier than up. Figured it'd be warmer in the valley. At least I'd survive for a time."

He passed by the first of the pools, steaming and tinged a pink liquid. He peered into the rosy water, catching only a glimpse of his own distorted reflection. As he neared the tree line, he thought he spotted something and perched himself atop an enormous boulder for a better look. But nothing moved in the distance, the trees as uniform and still as soldiers.

However, unknown to him, above and behind him, the first shadow climbed up to the edge of the pool and watched him, followed shortly by a second, then a third.

8

From Jack's viewpoint, a figure emerged from the trees. From this distance, it almost resembled a woman. A flicker of hope ignited in his eyes.

"I knew it. I'm not alone. Hey!" His shout pierced the silence, but the figure retreated further into the forest. Determined, Jack launched himself after it, his bulky orange jumpsuit contrasting against the muted landscape. "Hey, wait up. Hold on there!"

Despite the bulky suit, he sprinted over boulders and around the steaming pools, his agility surprising him.

Unbeknownst to him, three shadows descended the ragged slope above him, their movements stealthy and deliberate. However, they were not quite adept at negotiating the harsh terrain. They seemed to glow slightly in the descending dusk and continued to close in on Jack.

Jack burst into the undergrowth, the speed at which he moved startling even himself. He quickly overtook the tiny fleeing creature, bringing it down to the ground in a moist bed of ferns. Looking at the creature, which bore a resemblance to a small child, Jack's face lit up with excitement.

"Who are you? What are you? Talk to me?" he pleaded.

The creature, Alysa, managed to utter a single word, "Men."

"That's it? Men? Men what?" Jack pressed, his eyes wide with curiosity. Alysa struggled under him, finally managing to get up. The creature was beautiful, the only word that could accurately describe it. It had large, warm eyes, a small mouth, and barely-there ears.

Standing about five feet tall, Alysa was humanoid but asexual, looking delicate compared to Jack's bulkiness. Its skin was nearly translucent, appearing to glow from within.

"Meta fel maxsik hey Alysa. (In this world, they call me Alysa.)" Alysa said.

Jack stared, then started to laugh. "What are you saying?"

But Alysa's stare bore into him, making it clear that what was said was important.

"What's that supposed to mean?" Jack demanded. But Alysa turned and moved away. He grabbed Alysa, spinning the creature around and knocking it off balance again. They both landed back on the ground, but Jack pinned Alysa down this time.

"Just who are you anyway?" Jack's question was met with silence. "What are you?" he pressed, growing firm.

"Sefot! (Asshole!)" Alysa retorted.

Jack eased his grip. "Okay. It's okay. I'm not going to hurt you. I'm sorry. Really. It's okay."

Suddenly, a hand touched Jack's shoulder from behind, startling him.

"Men. (No.)" A new voice broke the silence, and Jack looked up at another creature, Sy. Smaller and just as delicate as Alysa, Sy somehow seemed older, more mature. The gentle kindness in Sy's eyes was so convincing that Jack immediately released Alysa.

"Fenty pal tara dexakiya. Men lax apad. (Let us go. We have

nothing for you.)" Sy spoke softly, words lost on Jack but the intention clear.

Jack watched, speechless, as Alysa rose to its feet.

"Alysa... stado. (Alysa, Shadows.)" Sy's voice was filled with an eerie warning. The two creatures began to move away slowly, then they vanished as suddenly as they had appeared. Left alone again, Jack stood in silence. When he finally gathered his thoughts, he noticed his hands were shaking.

"*I wanted to go back to being alone. Seeing these two beings sent a chill to my soul. I wanted to run away. I knew this was just the beginning,*" Jack whispered to the emptiness around him.

The morning sun found Jack by a stream in the richly vegetated forest of Gyon. The humidity was intense, causing him to sweat heavily. A good two feet thick, the moss climbed the trunks of gigantic trees that seemed to breathe life into the forest.

Blue droplets sprinkled from leaf to leaf like honey, creating a soft melody throughout the forest. The brook raced along, alive and boisterous.

Relishing the coolness of the stream, Jack rolled up his jumpsuit legs, ditched his boots, and waded into the water.

Singing, "*Just a little sunshine early in the morning. Just a little dip to brighten up the day. Just a little...*" His tune was abruptly cut off by a sudden hush in the forest. Jack looked around, his eyes finding nothing out of place.

"Sun," he muttered, the silence growing disturbing. He knew he was exposed in the stream and began to climb out, pulling his boots back on.

"Shine," he muttered as he zipped up his overalls. His heart pounded as he suddenly spotted a shadow less than twenty feet away. It rotated into view, followed by a second, and then a third. They were paper-thin, like androids. Jack grappled with these odd, two-dimensional beings. Their forms expanded and contracted, growing thick and thin,

More appeared around a bend in the stream. Three more backed up the first set. Jack was surrounded. Like faceless cops, the Shadows advanced in unison, closing in on the stream. They stopped just a few feet away, looking Jack over.

"Stamyna fex! (Don't move!)" one of them commanded.

Tension filled the air as Jack shuffled around, finding himself encircled. The shadowy figures were closing in, and he saw no immediate escape.

"Hemkavkra sed pagf mexraksik. (I think he's drunk.)" One shadow murmured.

"Misda misda anvaky. (Probably a poacher, too.)" The other responded. They nodded to each other, their soles casting a faint glow on the lush grass beneath them.

"Hey, hold on there. Just one minute. Who are you?" Jack challenged.

In response, the figures moved in, prodding him. As they did, Jack lashed out, knocking the foremost shadow to the ground. Yet, this did not deter the others. They seized him, pulling him back. A scuffle ensued on the ground, six other figures merely watching as he fought them, making their uncanny dimension all the more difficult to battle. A sharp kick to his ribs and, finally, Jack exploded with fury.

Singling out the leader, he brutally folded the creature over, snapping it in half before stomping it into the ground. The fight abruptly ceased. The remnants of the defeated creature fluttered like the wings of an ancient insect.

Seeing their fallen comrade, the other Shadows, who had seemed far more formidable than Jack, backed away. They gathered up the broken fragments, murmuring amongst themselves in what Jack could only interpret as concern.

"Pef. (One down, two to go.)"

"Men pef. Fel medo. (Forget it.)"

"Men medo. Bem? (You got a better answer?)"

"Fyrapo. (Checkmate. Sonofabitch!)"

With a seemingly shared agreement, the Shadows vanished, their speed indicative of fear.

"Fyrapo?" Jack queried, panting.

"Yes, that's right," came a voice from behind. Jack turned to see Sy, Alysa, and a third being nearby.

"You speak English?" he asked, astounded.

The three beings nodded, seemingly pleased by his recognition.

"Yes," Alysa confirmed, touching its lips. "I am Alysa." The being gestured towards the older figure, Sy, who introduced himself.

"And I am Sy."

The third figure, fair-skinned and oddly appealing to Jack, repeated the action. A soft glow emanated from within its body. "Call me Hym."

"You don't look like a him," Jack retorted. Alysa was quick to correct him.

"Hym, not him."

"If she's a guy, I'd like to see what the women in this place look like," Jack muttered, causing Alysa to shake its head, realizing Jack misunderstood.

"You've got it all wrong, Jack," Alysa clarified.

With a hearty laugh, Jack introduced himself, "I'm Jack. How can you speak English so well?"

"We watched you. We listened. We learned," Sy explained.

"In five minutes?"

"Less," Sy retorted, causing Jack to laugh again. The alien beings mirrored his laughter, their smiles broadening as if they'd just discovered long-lost kin.

Impressed and intrigued, Alysa extended a hand, beckoning Jack to cross the stream to their side. Upon his leap across, they exchanged handshakes.

"Well, where the hell am I, the moon?" Jack wondered aloud, evoking amusement from Alysa. After shaking hands with Hym and Sy, Sy turned and shook hands with Alysa, then Alysa with Hym, mimicking Jack's actions.

Seeming to understand, Hym nodded. "Ah, the moon. Thank you."

"So, who knows the way back to Earth?" Jack asked. Sy shook Jack's hand again, a knowing look in his eyes.

"What's the hurry?"

"Isn't this better than being dead?" Alysa chimed in.

"Well, yeah. Sort of," Jack admitted.

The forest came alive again with the sound of trickling plants, a chorus of bullfrogs croaking in unison, followed by the sudden appearance of a colorful, two-dimensional beast. It cavorted joyously around the group and through the stream, enjoying strokes from Alysa and Hym. Alysa introduced the creature.

"This is Budf. A pet."

"Budf... nice dog. I used to have a sheepdog like that," Jack said as the beast nuzzled his leg, its two-dimensional flatness startling. "Well, almost like that."

9

The tiny group crossed the forest floor in the soft steel-blue light filtering through the thick green foliage. The gentle lilac mist drifting in the air gave the surrounding verdant wilderness an ethereal quality. Dewdrops clung to the gigantic ferns, their sparkle creating a rich tapestry of a soft, emerald world that enveloped the travelers as they traversed the dark red sand.

The path they trod on was sparsely adorned with ground vegetation. Still, the trees reaching skyward, their roots winding haphazardly up from the ground, were immense and unlike anything found on Earth. Jack was fascinated by the strange landscape, his eyes following the flight of giant butterfly-like creatures that Budf enthusiastically chased, leaping up in an attempt to catch them.

As they journeyed further, they were dwarfed by perfectly formed semi-circular bushes of dense greenery. The red sand was flat, the bushes spaced evenly apart. It was a geometric pattern of red and green as if formed by a natural yet unfa-miliar force. Jack glanced around, awed by the repeating pattern of red paths winding around the enormous green hemi-spheres of plant life.

The journey led them over a gentle knoll, the grassy hill offering a view of the incredible landscape stretching below them. A glistening lake was nestled amid a series of rolling hills, and off to one side, sheltered by a grove of colossal Wilpelm trees, Jack could see the beginnings of a small camp. The group moved downhill, and after a moment's hesitation, Jack followed.

The camp comprised three small crystalline tetrahedra hidden under a canopy of willowy branches from the trees. One of the shelters appeared complete, while the other two were still under construction, suggesting a sense of imperma-nence for the beings.

"You live here?" Jack asked, glancing at Alysa.

She nodded in response.

Jack gazed at the idyllic scene, his voice laced with genuine admiration. "It's beautiful. Very peaceful."

The housing units were modest in size, standing no more than six feet high. Their sides were opaque, bathed in varying soft pastel hues. Entry was gained through an opening located at the corner of each structure. Essential items were scattered about a shaded space in the center of the layout, contributing to a pleasing sense of tranquility, privacy, and seclusion that the camp exuded.

"What were those things back there?" Jack inquired.

"Shadows. They are dangerous," Sy replied.

"Shadows, huh?" Jack echoed, raising his eyebrows.

"They work for an Enforcer named Xyrak. Xyrak has made Fyrapo part of our life," Alysa added.

"Fyrapo? What is that?" Jack asked, puzzled.

The others exchanged glances. "Life. The ultimate game. The only game," Sy finally explained. He gestured for Jack to sit and emptied a small cloth bag onto the ground. Dozens of colored polished tetrahedra tumbled out. Sy separated the colors, handing Jack twenty-one amber pieces.

Three differentiated crystals were arranged by Sy in a triangular formation around an open center on the ground.

"Just a game?" Jack asked, looking at the pieces in his hand.

"What isn't?" Sy retorted, motioning for Jack to place a piece next to his own. Jack complied, watching as Sy adjusted it, aligning it with some larger invisible boundary. Hym joined in, placing a cameo pink crystal next to Jack's amber one.

"What are the rules?"

"You'll see."

"And what are the stakes?" Jack inquired, intrigued.

"Your life," Sy responded simply.

"Good. I didn't bring any money," Jack jested, watching intently as Sy placed a carbon black tetrahedron next to a pink one.

The game proceeded quickly, with each player adding pieces to the formation. Very soon, all sixty-three crystals were in place, forming a triangular matrix. The sunlight reflecting off the pattern dispersed a rainbow of color.

"Why is the center empty? Don't tell me," Jack asked, looking at the void in the formation.

"Your move," Sy simply replied.

"So, this is what advanced civilizations do in their spare time? You know I've always wondered that," Jack mused, taking his amber piece to jump a pink one and remove it from the board. A broad smile spread across his face.

The game continued with pieces being jumped and removed. Eventually, Hym stopped and stood up, prompting Jack to ask, "Where are you going? You still have some pieces left. She still has some pieces left, right?"

"No," Sy answered, shaking his head.

Confused, Jack turned to Hym, "Oh sure, girls get to cheat. Your daughters?" Jack asked, winking at Sy. Sy responded by placing a finger on its lips.

10

"Go ahead and move," Sy urged Jack.

"Sy, can I be honest with you?" Jack replied, looking baffled. "I'm confused. I jumped out of an airplane, and I landed in a blizzard. I thought I was dead. And now I'm playing Chinese checkers with a couple of dwarfs. No offense, of course, but isn't there any nightlife here?"

He jumped a pink piece and captured Sy's black one. Sy, however, stopped him. "What's an airplane?" Sy inquired, a puzzled expression on his face.

"What do you mean what's an airplane? It's a thing that flies. You know, fly," Jack retorted, his eyebrows furrowing.

"Fly? We can fly. You have one move left," Sy responded casually. He replaced the captured carbon crystal, moved Jack's amber piece back, and held up one finger.

"You have airplanes?" Jack asked, surprised.

"Only one," Sy replied.

"Where is it?" Jack pressed.

Before Sy could reply, Alysa stepped in, holding up one finger. "One, Jack," she reiterated.

"Fine. One airplane is fine. I stopped flying two at the same time when I gave up wing walking," Jack retorted, a smirk on his face.

Alysa touched Jack's shoulder, putting a finger to her lips. "Just move," she instructed.

"Rebel in me," he responded, jumping another piece. The game continued until it was clear that Jack had more pieces left and more captured than Sy or Hym. Excited, he jumped up. "Piece of cake. Where's my prize?"

"Prize?" Sy asked, looking puzzled.

"On Wheel of Fortune, I won a washer-dryer, and I only had to guess an 'L,'" Jack said, smirking as he surveyed the remaining crystals.

"Sy, just admit you've been whipped and let me borrow your cell phone, that is, if you still use them," he said aloud. Sy simply took another move, removing one of Jack's amber pieces.

"What's a cell phone?" Sy asked, appearing intrigued.

"It's the ultimate toy. With 5G, you can Facetime anyone in the world," Jack explained, grinning.

"What's 5G?" Sy asked.

"That's how I look at it," Jack replied, looking over the board. To his dismay, he realized he had no moves left.

"Look, I have ten. Each of you has three. Sorry. Pay up," Jack insisted, turning back to Sy.

"Fyrapo," was all Sy said in response.

"Fyrapo? What do you mean? So who wins?" Jack asked, flustered.

"Move," Alysa encouraged him, challenging him to make a final move.

"As soon as I collect, I will," Jack shot back, an edge in his voice. Alysa simply smiled in response.

"Fyrapo," she said again, her eyes sparkling with amusement and victory.

All my instincts were wrong. Sure, you jumped pieces and

removed them like checkers from the board. But Fyrapo was more. It was survival. Constant movement. You stop moving, and you're dead and out of the game. To win Fyrapo, you had to make the last move, Jack thought, his gaze meeting Sy's.

Inside the crystalline shelter, Jack's exhaustion finally took over. He retreated toward the entrance, observing the beings outside as they went about their tasks. He was interrupted by a high-pitched whine that filled the air. Sy, Alysa, and Hym each held a crystal in their hands, weaving a thickening substance that completed the incomplete crystalline structures. Alysa, in particular, was tinting one side blue.

Later, Jack roused from a brief sleep and exited his shelter. The beings seemed to pay him no mind. The twin moons spiraled off into the horizon and disappeared from sight.

Alysa approached him with a curious look in her eyes. She was eyeing the transmitter still affixed to Jack's chest. "What is this?" she asked, poking it.

"Radio transmitter," Jack replied, a hint of irritation in his voice.

"What does it do?" Alysa questioned further.

"With this, everyone in the whole world can hear me," he stated, a hint of pride in his voice. "If they have a radio."

"Radio?"

"Crystal, crystal radio."

"Why?" Alysa queried, her confusion evident.

Before Jack could reply, a singular chamois moon traced its orbit across the lavender-green sky. High above the tree line beyond the lake, the other two twin bodies began their ascent into the molten heavens. It was an everyday sight for Alysa, but Jack couldn't tear his gaze away from the spectacle. But he felt dejected and lost, realizing but not accepting his predicament.

"Look, just leave me alone. I don't want to talk anymore. I

need to get my thoughts straight," Jack finally said, his voice fraught with frustration.

Back inside his crystalline shelter, Jack finally succumbed to his exhaustion. As he slept, the filtered colors from outside painted a brilliant prism of light across his unshaven face. Suddenly, Budf licked him and, seeming frightened, dashed out of the shelter.

Outside, Budf sprinted into the forest. Alysa called after him, "Budf, come back here." A painful howl pierced the air, followed by terrified screams. Alysa was about to chase after the pet, but Sy held her back. "Alysa, wait."

Almost as soon as Sy had uttered the warning, a menacing troop of shadows marched over the hill toward them. The tranquility of the camp was shattered, replaced with an air of fear. The shadows' formation was impressive, and their movement was military-like. They blinked in and out of existence as they crossed the crest, rotating in units of fifty.

The lead formation halted about sixty feet from the small group. The Leader directed their attention across the lake. Jack, awakened by the commotion, stumbled out of bed. The chilling cry of the screaming creature still echoed in their ears as Sy, Alysa, and Hym looked out over the water.

11

Their eyes were drawn to the far shore of the still, blue lake, where a brilliant white light began to burn a pocket in the forest. A high-speed hiss filled the air, growing louder and resonating across the lake. The tiny flaming ball charged toward them, warping the surrounding landscape and creating a sense that time had ceased to exist.

An explosive pop shattered the tranquility right before them. The light retracted into nothingness, giving way to ten highly decorated Chief Shadows. From this ominous group, their leader, Xyrak, emerged. The being was magnetic, regal, and struck an imposing figure. Ignoring Sy and the others, Xyrak commanded the forces into action.

"Raid the shelters. Destroy anyone who gets in your way," Xyrak commanded, speaking in a language foreign to Jack's ears.

The Shadows descended on the camp, thoroughly searching the shelters. Amidst the commotion, Xyrak and the key team stood still, their calm contrasting with the chaos. Sy and the others were held at bay, overpowered by the legions. Jack watched, stunned and confused by their forceful presence.

When the search turned up nothing, Xyrak initiated a final move. The shelters cracked apart with each touch, yet before any piece fell to the ground, it vanished. When Sy moved to interfere, Xyrak glared at him, the being's voice smooth, controlled, and intimidating.

"Old master, so proud you would save this one?" Xyrak asked, showing an almost aristocratic demeanor.

Sy remained silent, refusing to answer. Undeterred, Xyrak proceeded, bringing into play a greater power that caused the shelter to burst apart in blue flame, scorching the ground. Xyrak emerged from the wreckage unscathed.

Jack watched helplessly while Sy, Alysa, and Hym looked deeply disturbed. The disappointment and disgust in Xyrak's eyes spoke volumes. Turning to Sy, Xyrak said a single word: "Gyon."

"It's still here," Sy responded.

"Is it? Why are you thinking like this?" Xyrak queried before turning to two chief shadows and commanding, "Pick them up!"

In compliance, the Shadows confiscated the group's crystals. Jack protested, moving to stop them, but found Xyrak blocking his path. Xyrak appeared amused by Jack's appearance and the black box on his chest.

"Excuse me? Some problem?" Xyrak inquired, unthreatened by Jack's stature.

"No," Jack responded, backing off, which seemed to satisfy Xyrak.

With a quick toss, the crystals vanished into the sky, never to land. Xyrak gave a final command, "Fex Lavana," and Sy was seized.

"Hold on there. Just one minute," Jack protested, but before he could react further, there was a hard flash of light. Xyrak and the Chief Shadows vanished from sight, taking Sy with them. Only Jack's echo remained.

The hissing glow sped across the lake, ascending into the

discolored sky. Jack stood there, awe-struck. As he turned around, he realized the shadows had retreated. A dull, harmonic thunder pounded in the distance. The unnerving cries from the forest suddenly ceased, leaving an eerie silence behind.

Moments later, Jack, Hym, and Alysa stood unharmed but shaken by the abrupt loss. Of the three, Jack was the only one who showed discernible distress.

"What's going on here? I don't understand any of this. You two just going to let him do this to you?" Jack demanded, his voice echoing his confusion and frustration.

Hym and Alysa exchanged a few quick, whispered phrases before addressing Jack. The serious look in their eyes indicated the gravity of the situation.

"Xyrak made the last move," Hym said, its voice steady but laced with apprehension.

"He just kidnapped Sy and destroyed your homes. What are you talking about, last move? That's bullshit," Jack protested, not understanding their cryptic words.

Alysa's eyes, filled with a slow-burning rage, were fixated on the now-placid lake. There was an intense determination in her gaze that was impossible to miss. Hym fell silent, unable to respond. Alysa knew what was next.

"In ways never before seen, we will defeat this enforcer once and for all," she vowed, her voice decisive and resolute.

"Alright," Jack finally responded, resigning himself to the unfamiliar situation.

The landscape of Gyon lay bleak under the fading twin moons. Their maroon glow left the clouded sky, leaving only the sun locked in its early morning position. A world that did not rotate, its blazing yellow sun cast a striking contrast against the expanse of unfocused green.

Three solitary figures traversed the rich, emerald terrain of a lush rainforest.

I felt like Adam naming the world," Jack's voice echoed in a voiceover, painting a picture of his inner turmoil. "*The forest was Gyon. The game was Fyrapo. But two-dimensional Shadows and a man who could disappear in a flash of light? That didn't make sense. It was like running into a huge Bugs Bunny cartoon. I thought I liked cartoons until now.*

A quiet knoll stood before them. Jack, leading Alysa and Hym over the grassy crest through the magnificent forest, began to sing softly, perhaps to distract himself or to lift his spirits.

"This land is your land. This land is my land, from California to the New York Island."

Hym came to an abrupt halt.

"What's wrong?" Alysa queried, a note of concern creeping into her voice.

"There is only one thing left," Hym replied, a hint of resignation tinting its voice.

"I know. We have to go back," Alysa acknowledged with determination.

"I don't want to go back," Hym retorted, its opposition evident.

"Hym, we have no choice. Without crystals, without Sy, we have nothing," Alysa reasoned.

"Wrong. By going, we destroy everything we have and believe in," Hym argued.

"We're saving Sy. What's more important than that?" Alysa challenged, her conviction unwavering.

"Girls, look, what's the matter? What's the problem? We don't want to bring the U.N. into this," Jack interjected, trying to defuse the situation.

"Put a lid on it, Jack," Hym snapped, clearly irritated.

"Jeez, you do learn fast," Jack muttered, slightly taken aback.

"Hym," Alysa softly implored, reaching out to the recalcitrant figure.

Unfazed, Jack whistled the tune to "This land was made for you and me." He tried to infuse some cheer into the tense atmosphere.

"Everybody now, alright? This land, come on... this land is..." he prompted, a forced cheerfulness in his tone.

"Alarym," Alysa responded, distracted from her tense conversation with Hym.

Hym still hesitated, unwilling to give in just yet.

"Your land. This land is..." Jack continued his song, a hint of desperation coloring his tone.

"Hym, I have no choice. Sy's my father. Sy's a master. Please?" Alysa pleaded, her voice tinged with worry and desperation.

With a deep sigh, Hym took a step in the right direction.

"My land. Alright! This land was made for you and me," Jack exulted, relief evident in his voice.

12

As the sun began to set, deep into the forest, the hapless trio trudged along a ravaged path. Broken branches, fragments of winter root and witch hazel, oleander, and sage littered the ground. The forest that once echoed harmony now sang a tune of discord. It seemed as though the forest had a mind and sensitivity of its own, its melody now a forbidding tempest chewed up and twisted by the army of Shadows.

By dusk, they found themselves by a stream in the heart of the forest of Gyon, preparing to ford the surging brook. A grim cocktail of blight, pond scum, ergot, and bracken bubbled in the surge.

"You sure we're going the right way?" Jack asked, casting a dubious glance around.

"There's only one way back," Alysa responded, her eyes never leaving the path ahead.

"I could have sworn little Napoleon went the other way. Over the lake." Jack voiced his confusion, but Alysa simply moved closer to him. Hym took a position on Jack's other side, leading to a flattered smile from Jack, intrigued by the unusual attention.

"Krosda, Jack. Krosda," Alysa repeated.

"Krosda?" Jack queried, puzzled. The forest around them was eerily still. Alysa placed her hands across Jack's chest, her soft, warm eyes staring into his, glowing with an inner fire. With a finger to her lips, she commanded delicate silence.

As twilight fell, they ventured deeper into the forest. The terrain darkened, the vegetation thickened, and strange colors refracted off the marshy ground, creating patches of gray and black. Moss draped the landscape like thick caterpillar worms. Sphagnum, club moss, Spanish and white, all creating a canvas of gray-green fantasy beneath their feet.

A light drizzle began to fall as Jack struggled to find a clear path through the vegetation, prompting him to jest, "A little rain this evening on the big clock, KLOQ. Get those wipers on and watch for oil on the freeway. I'll be back on the half-hour, and here's Alysa with the news."

Alysa and Hym looked at him, puzzled. Jack laughed, then stumbled into a thick ooze. A lightning bolt tore through the greenwood, cracking a branch that fell, exploding into flame. The branch landed amongst rotting undergrowth, belching up thick black smoke.

With thunderclaps overhead, Hym and Alysa rushed for cover. But Jack was nowhere to be seen.

"Jack? Jack?" Alysa called out as the rain intensified.

"Hym, where's Jack?" Alysa asked, her voice filled with concern.

"Jack quit fooling around!" Alysa cried, her voice barely audible over the roar of the storm.

Lightning bolts ripped through the shrubs, plunging huge

gaping holes into the sides of trees. A shower of sparks surged off one tree, mixed with the rain, and ignited a bed of floating moss clusters. The forest was ablaze, and the storm's fury was yet to break.

Night had taken hold, and Jack struggled below the storm-tossed surface of the lake. Weeds coiled around his legs, dragging him deeper into a watery abyss. The glow of fire above the water's surface was his only guide, but it was shrinking fast. As lightning zapped into the water from above, he fought against the weeds that seemed intent on pulling him down to his doom.

He shouted, the sound distorted by the seabed and his growing fear. Jack relaxed, straining to free his legs, but the current was unyielding. It spun him, towing him deeper. He aimed for the heart of the whirlpool, the maelstrom washing him into a stream of bubbles. He slammed into solid rock, was dragged along a ledge, and spat out into a calmer pocket of water just as the last of his breath escaped him.

He gasped, swallowing the slimy water as he drifted in the gloom. A flicker of light caught his eye. Without a second thought, his hands pulled him along the ledge, inch by inch, toward salvation.

A thick beam of light split the water like a rope in an underwater cavern. Smaller beams surrounded it, shattering the surface as Jack's head emerged from the depths. He found himself inside a cave. The cavern was small, an air pocket no larger than a room. Coughing and spitting, Jack clawed his way to the cavern wall. His wet transmitter was pulling him down.

With a last surge of strength, he unstrapped the transmitter from his chest and placed it onto the moist rock ledge. Every breath he took caused the needle on the transmitter's meter to jump, encased in its waterproof case.

"I guess this is it. If you haven't heard me now. You probably never will. If this ever gets back to Earth, just remember that

Jack Bradford was here in 2023," Jack murmured. He looked at the meter needle, fluttering in response to his words.

The cavern echoed with the drip of water. Pings and plips bounced off the walls. It was a sound Jack would never forget. With a last gulp of air, he plunged back underwater.

A current of pink water in the surrounding darkness led him on. Huge pink flowers from a fallen tree washed into a network of underwater caves. Jack, orange and slimy, pulled himself along the rocks, caught in the tumultuous stream. Lightning crackled overhead, thunder rocked the ground, and rain hammered down. He found his way to shore.

Alysa and Hym appeared, their figures outlined against the stormy backdrop. They looked down at Jack, a blot of pink and orange in the thick, mossy stream. The two stepped into the water to help him.

As Jack stumbled to his knees, the rain pounded down, drenching them all. Jack tried to smile, his face a mix of relief and joy. But Alysa's eyes widened as she noticed the water on Jack's cheek was coming from within. Gently, Alysa touched a teardrop, and her confusion mingled with relief.

13

———

Emerging from the forest, Jack, Alysa, and Hym started the long, steep climb through a canyon, a rough scar on the land connecting two disparate worlds. Jack's empty chest slot drew Alysa's curious gaze.

"What's the matter?" Jack asked, following Alysa's gaze to his chest.

"I got rid of it. No one's listening anyway," he confessed, though Alysa didn't fully understand.

They pressed on, ascending, helping Hym navigate some more challenging ledges. Along the way, they traversed fields of black ash, plowing through the powdery remnants of the once-vibrant landscape.

"How did this happen?" Jack asked, surveying the charred remnants of trees and accumulated ash. Alysa and Hym exchanged knowing glances but remained silent.

"It couldn't have changed this much. So quickly." Jack argued.

"Yes, like the forest," Alysa responded simply.

"Shadows," Hym added cryptically.

"Shadows? What is this place?" Jack questioned.

"Shadow Run," Alysa informed him. Without further explanation, they pressed on, Jack trailing them through the icy sleet and hail.

Finally, they sought shelter within an ice passage. With uncertainty clinging to their every step, they skidded and slid along the icy passageway as darkness crept in. Using the sheer walls for support, they clung to each other, crawling on hands and knees through the narrow openings. Their feet sloshed through a thin layer of black dust infiltrating the tunnel.

"It's going to be freezing up here. Isn't there some other way?" Jack's voice echoed against the icy walls.

"It's the only path between Gyon and Alarym," Alysa countered with a touch of certainty.

"You're sure?" Jack's doubt hung in the air, but Hym answered confidently. "We're sure."

They stumbled out of the claustrophobic passageway into a cavern that took their breath away. In a large phosphorus cavern, warm green steam spewed from the depths below, billowing forth in emerald hues like a pencil sketch of cascading black lines. Hym and Alysa quickly covered up, pulling the hoods on their garments over their heads.

"You alright?" Jack asked, but neither responded.

The sound of coughing filled the space, followed by a sneeze. Both Alysa and Hym turned to Jack. Sneezing was a foreign concept to them.

"It's nothing. Probably just a little pneumonia. We get it all the time where I come from," Jack tried to dismiss it, but they watched him silently. "Ah choo."

Alysa smiled.

"It's a bit like a steam room in here, huh? Clears you out," Jack attempted to break the silence, but it only deepened. "The storm will probably pass real soon, you think?"

No response came, just the quiet puffing of the emerald-lined steam. It was Hym who moved to Jack, looking deeply into his eyes.

Hym, in a rare display, unveiled a vibrant leg and the crystalline lining of its robe. It looked intently at Jack. "Shadows," Hym said simply.

"Here?" Jack asked.

"Outside," Hym clarified.

With a nod from Hym and Jack got up, disappearing into the thick green mist. Alysa tried to reassure Hym in Jack's absence. "Don't worry. He'll be okay," but Hym only shook its head.

"We'll find Sy. You'll see," Alysa promised, but the reply was disheartening.

"Nothing will change," said Hym.

Alysa stared at its friend, frustration seeping into her features. "It's all part of Fyrapo. You know that."

Venturing out into the storm, Jack soon reappeared through the emerald steam, his eyes dark and watery from the heavy mist. He caught the whispering pair and headed over to them, coughing intermittently. "No Shadows around. But I saw a tunnel farther up. I think we can climb up inside it and stay warm."

"Let's do it," Alysa agreed, but Hym was reluctant. "I want to go back."

"We can't. You know that," Alysa reasoned, eyes filled with worry, but Hym stood firm and voiced its fear. "You're wrong. I can."

"Alone? We've got nothing out there. You wouldn't survive a day without Sy," Alysa countered.

"I think I can," Hym persisted. The group stopped in their tracks.

Despite Alysa's reassurances, Hym remained doubtful. Yet, they had no choice but to continue into the unknown.

"Tunnel looks real good. I think it'll be safer than out there," Jack announced, trying to deflect from the tense exchange. Alysa unexpectedly reached out and grabbed Jack's hand. He didn't pull away.

"What about her, Hym? Whatever," Jack said, vague confusion etched across his face. Alysa vanished into the swirling leaf-green mist.

"Jack, if I return to Alarym with you, they will make things very unpleasant," Hym warned.

"More unpleasant than out there?" Jack asked.

"Worse. If you were smart, you wouldn't go. Once you get in, you can never get out," Hym retorted before leaving Jack and heading back.

Hym, alone by the entrance of the ice tunnel, peered out at the raging storm. The icy pellets blasted the landscape, creating an eerie moan from the mountain. The warmth radiating from the ice caves seemed inviting in comparison. After long consideration, Hym took a few uncertain steps and reentered the Irish mist.

In the dim twilight of the ice tunnel, three Shadows emerged, eerily quiet, as they listened to the echoes in the fog. They waited.

Finding a fork in the path ahead, Hym descended the wrong tunnel. She stopped suddenly, removing its hood. Eyes wide, lost, Hym looked around, only to be met with the ominous sight of the Shadows. One of them produced a bright red crystal and pointed it at her. As the beam hit her, she collapsed.

· · ·

Meanwhile, Jack and Alysa navigated a frozen passage, arriving at a thick ice wall.

"Dead end. What if all the tunnels are blocked like this?" Jack fretted.

"We'll try another one," Alysa suggested optimistically.

"And if that's blocked?"

"We'll try another," Alysa repeated, her determination unwavering.

Jack and Alysa descended along the left path through the swirling mist of the ice tunnel, rounding a corner only to be met with a shocking sight. Hym was standing within a transparent ice wall, alive but visibly trapped. Communication was futile, sound muffled by the ice.

"Come on. We have to get her out. She'll freeze to death," Jack declared, taking a few steps toward the icy prison.

Alysa watched with an air of detachment as Jack launched himself at the ice wall, his strikes reverberating within the tunnel. His fists and shoulders did little to budge the icy barrier despite his determination. He left briefly, reappearing moments later with a brittle branch in hand. He jabbed at the wall, only to find the ice unyielding. With a sigh, he pressed his hand against the wall.

"It's not ice. It's something else," he stated, a note of perplexity in his voice.

From within her icy confinement, Hym gestured at them. Alysa turned, taking a few steps away.

"Alysa, where are you going? We can't just leave her here," Jack shouted, his eyes wide with disbelief.

Alysa paused, looking back at him. "Fyrapo, Jack," she said simply.

"I don't care about Fyrapo. You can't just let her die," Jack retorted, desperation edging his voice.

"She won't die. In Fyrapo, nobody ever dies," Alysa replied cryptically before vanishing into the phosphorous-green mist.

Jack turned his gaze back to Hym, trying to make sense of her silent warnings. "Shadow?" he asked, seeking confirmation. Hym nodded and then seated herself, a picture of quiet resignation.

"You're wrong, Hym. You can't just give up like that. We'll come back for you. You hear me. You can't give up," Jack declared, his words echoing in the icy tunnel.

With one final punch at the wall, he turned and disappeared into the green steam.

Moments later, a figure materialized within the tunnel. Statuesque, dark, and eerily silent, it was a shadow.

14

In the unchanging landscape of a planet locked in a strange rotation, the twilight beauty of dawn and dusk never graced the land. Jack and Alysa trudged across an endless expanse of ice under the watchful gaze of the first of Gyon's twin moons. It played a haunting game of peekaboo through the maroon clouds, casting an ethereal glow over the snow-laden terrain.

A gust of frigid wind struck Jack in the face, drawing out a cough from his raspy throat. His sneezing fit ended with a slam against his chest.

"This dry cough and this nagging, aching feeling. I should try Advil," he muttered.

"Why are you making those sounds?" Alysa asked, laying a hand on his chest and curiously eyeing her companion.

"Colds, it's something we humans get on nights like this. I suppose you don't," Jack replied, coughing again.

"You're right. We don't," Alysa confirmed.

"Well, maybe that's because you're more advanced than we are," Jack reasoned, grinning despite his discomfort.

"You're probably right," Alysa agreed, mimicking a cough in jest.

"Think it's funny? This is not funny," Jack retorted, hacking into his fist. Alysa merely tilted her head to the side and poked his chest, eliciting a groan from him.

"You shouldn't have thrown away your toy box," she teased.

Their journey led them across frozen ice floes, hopping from one to another as the cyan waters below mirrored the twirling dance of Gyon's twin moons. When they finally reached firm ground, the moons traced rapid arcs through the maroon sky, outpacing their singular sibling.

Jack looked up at a thinning cloud cover revealing a sky teeming with stars. He scanned the celestial bodies, seeking familiarity amidst the strange constellations.

"Do you know where we are? I mean, where we really are?" he asked Alysa, his eyes darting across the starscape.

"That star is Akalapy, the next Tryka. The constellation is in the galaxy Fantym," Alysa supplied, pointing out a couple to him.

Jack's eyes widened. "Phantom? Look again. Don't you see what that is? It's the Dipper, the Big Dipper? I'm not so lost after all." His joy was palpable, filling the cold night air with a whoop of triumph. But his elation was short-lived.

"Wait a second," Jack muttered, gazing at the star pattern. He paled, looking bewildered. "Alysa, it's the wrong way around."

In the silent expanse of the night, his revelation hung heavily. The familiar yet strange constellations presented a reality he struggled to comprehend. His solitariness enveloped him, and he muttered to himself, his words carried away by the wind.

"If it's the wrong way around here, then that means I'm on

the other side. Holy shit! I'm not on this side. I'm on that side. --
That's impossible. That means I'm down there. How can that
be? I'll never get back."

Overwhelmed, Jack sank to his knees, despair etched on his
face. "God, please, tell me. What did I do to deserve this? Am I
such a bad guy? Beth... I wish you were here."

His anguish echoed into the night, and a cold wind
answered him, dusting his frozen hands with fine snow. But
amid the desolation, a soft voice punctured the quiet.

"Jack?"

Alysa knelt beside him, draping part of her gown over his
hands and pulling him into a gentle embrace. She offered no
words, only her comforting presence in the heart of the alien
night.

A soft glow bristled in the air against the backdrop of the
mountainside. Thirty spotted caverns nestled in the mountain
ledge, each belching out warm, green smoke that solidified into
crystals in the night air. Crackling ice shattered the silence of
the dark, its fragments carving through the snow like miniature
blades. Another sound echoed in the quiet — Jack's harsh shivering and coughing as he followed Alysa toward the shelter of a
phosphorous cavern.

Inside, Alysa guided Jack towards the steaming warmth, her
large, tranquil eyes focused on him. The corners of her mouth
twitched upwards, hinting at an inner calm.

"Tell me about Alarym," Jack requested, his voice bouncing
off the cavern walls.

"It's like a city but more than a city. It is a state of mind.
Power and culture and magic," Alysa responded, her voice soft.

"And if you leave this city?"

"No one had tried before us."

"Why?"

"People were happy. We had everything."

"And now?"

"Some of us sense there's more, and you've confirmed it."

Their conversation was interrupted by the whistling of the wind and the unsettling rumble of the mountain. Jack turned towards Alysa, curiosity alight in his eyes.

"You know me, don't you?"

"In some ways, yes. Why?"

"I've never felt more comfortable with anyone in my life. I don't know what it is, but I feel like we've known each other for a very long time!" he said.

"We have. Only sometimes, we don't remember. I'm glad you came back."

Alysa moved away to block the entrance from the biting wind, her vigil silent and resolute. Meanwhile, Jack lay down, puzzled by Alysa's words, oblivious to a dark, thin object descending above him from the ice-covered ceiling.

Droplets of water fell onto his face, spurring him to wipe them away. The ice above continued to melt, giving way to a sudden eruption of milky fluid that drenched Jack's face and body. He barely had time to react before the dark object tumbled onto him, pinning him with its cold weight.

With a yelp, Jack scrambled to his feet, shaking. He found himself staring at the lifeless body of a being, dark, cold, dry, and blue, as though drained of all life. Alysa was instantly by his side, a mix of shock, recognition, and contempt flashing in her eyes.

"What is it? Who is it?" Jack asked, poking at the still, icy figure.

"Tythe," Alysa responded her voice, barely a whisper.

"You know him?" Jack inquired. Alysa nodded slowly. "My brother." For the first time, the alien being was confronted with death. For the first time, their world knew mortality.

Alysa glanced at Jack, her eyes almost accusing as she struggled to connect the man and the corpse. "Jack," she said, her tone cold.

Jack didn't understand her intention. He put his arms around her, comforting her. "He's dead, Alysa. Frozen to death. It could happen to anyone out here. Even us."

Alysa shook her head. "It can't. Not here."

Without another word, Alysa turned on her heel and bolted out of the cavern. "Alysa? Alysa!" Jack called out after her, but his only response was the cold air that blasted into the cavern. The steam within froze and fell to the ground.

The cat was out of the bag. I brought death to their world. They had never seen it before. It took me a long time to understand that. All she could do was to make it a part of Fyrapo, a game we were apparently losing, Jack reflected. His voice echoed in the desolate cavern, his revelation weighing heavily on him.

15

Between a cluster of boulders and a spew of black ash on the mountainside, Jack found a solitary, brittle tree, partially buried with a few upper branches protruding into the night like jagged veins. He snapped a twig off it and fashioned a cross, patting a handful of chipped ice on the newly formed grave.

"Rest in peace, Tythe," Jack murmured as he placed the handmade cross on the mound. Alysa observed quietly, her face an unreadable mask.

"What does 'rest in peace' mean?" Alysa asked, curiosity coloring her voice.

"It's a custom we have on Earth. When someone dies, we bury them. Ashes to ashes, dust to dust. Like that. Plant a cross, say a prayer," Jack explained.

"Prayer?"

"Yeah. We hope their soul lives on."

As Jack bowed his head and clasped his hands in prayer, Alysa mirrored his actions, her gaze intensely focused on him. Jack recited, "Our Father, which are in heaven, hallowed by Thy name." He paused, reconsidering his words, then added, "For thine is the kingdom, the power, and the glory. Amen."

Alysa echoed brightly, "Amen."

They traversed a narrow ledge on the mountainside, the treacherous journey made precarious by the vast gaps between footholds. A massive snow drift blocked their path at the ledge's end, which they dug through to reach a sheer ice shelf. An intimidating chasm separated them from their destination: the mountain summit on the way to Alarym.

With the wind furiously howling around them, Alysa estimated the jump across the chasm. In one swift motion, she leaped, landing safely on the other side. But as Jack prepared to follow, the ice beneath him collapsed. Trapped in mid-air, Jack was pummeled by a crashing overhang of snow and ice, swallowed up in a furious whiteout.

Now alone at the summit, Alysa called out, "Jack? Jack?" The only reply she received was her own echo reverberating around the snow-capped peak, swallowed by the rumbling mountain and the relentless wind. The harsh and desolate landscape looked as though no one had been here for hundreds of years.

Jack, caught in an avalanche, was buried deep underground. Beneath the snow, all he saw was white, a hazy suggestion of a shadow. His mind raced with memories of the past. *A charity event once taught me to swim with an avalanche. Like you swim with a wave. The problem was when the chips were down, I forgot all the survival stuff. Just tell me what this was all about, and I could die a happy man. The answer, as it turned out, was right under my nose.*

Separated by a thick transparent wall, he glimpsed a brilliant complex illuminated from within the mountain. The sight spurred him to action, and he found a way to force open a ceiling hatch leading to the portal below. Snow tumbled inside as the portal hatch swung open, and Jack carefully maneuvered his way down.

The symphony of dripping water echoed inside the mountain in a crystal maze. Balancing on a massive strut, Jack carefully crawled along with a trapeze artist's precision.

From his vantage point, he witnessed a small stream of snow trickling down through the portal, disappearing into the dazzling light hundreds of feet below. The sight was breathtaking. An enormous, elegant triangle of crystal and light, of motion and color, lay below. The transparent structure formed a labyrinth of dark and near-mystical beauty—a modern alien city encased within the mountain.

Taking his time, Jack shimmied along the strut, inching his way toward a bright red light in the distance.

The heart of the subterranean city was the Crystal Plaza, where a series of pink light stanchions circled an immense radiant fountain. Beings and creatures of all shapes and descriptions congregated in groups of three, their excitement palpable as a light dusting of snow from the portal opening fell over the transparent hilly area.

The sight was so mesmerizing that everyone halted their activities. Three shadows emerged from the crowd, stepping forward regimented, their feet emitting a soft glow. As they looked up into the unending darkness, the echoing sound of water drips seemed to unnerve them. When a second snow flurry reached them, they quickly collected samples, storing the white powder in cylindrical urns belted to their waists. After sealing their samples, they vanished as they turned in a true two-dimensional fashion.

Beyond the Crystal Plaza, a narrow, winding street, Moonstone Way, cut through a collection of golden beryl structures. Three artificial beings, known as Ghosts, roamed the road, their slender, pink forms searching for the source of the water drip sounds echoing off the slanted, tinted walls. A small, yellow creature scurried around a corner, and the Ghosts, dutiful as ever, followed it.

Prism Wynd, a nearby street, was a spectacle of light. Horizontal bands of colored light, ten feet high, raced along the path like a freeway of luminescence. Among this dazzling spectacle, an older being, Mystyl, was cautioning six small pets of assorted shades and colors—some resembling kittens, a chimpanzee, a dodo, an egret, and a coati—to stay to the side.

"Fex fex," Mystyl warned.

As the red band of light above them faded, and a whirl of spinning light spiraled past, the sound of the dripping water echoed in the distance. Mystyl spoke to the pets in a soft, familiar tone.

"Vyntektyka rys synyi Gyonial," Mystyl said, believing the legend of Gyon had finally come to pass.

16

—————

In the dimming twilight, Shadow Central hummed with activity. Twenty-one Shadows sat in exact rows of seven, reclining three deep, their glowing soles connected to the wall. Before each shadow was a lightboard dotted with colorful monitors. There were no operational dials, only a semi-circle filled with triangular faces, some colored, some not. Yet, no matter how hard they tried, none of the Shadows could tune out the dripping water's incessant plip, plop from Jack's radio transmitter.

When a light flickered on one unit, a door opened. Three Shadows marched forward, headed towards an elevated station, and disappeared into a short black corridor.

In the Operations Center, a triangular room surrounded by glass, Xyrak had a panoramic view of the entire complex. The three Shadows entered and approached a central table.

"Report. What did you find?" Xyrak commanded.

The Shadows unbelted the dark cylinders from their waists, tipping them over. Instead of the expected snowflakes, only a few drops of moisture fell onto the table with familiar sounds —plip, plik, plop.

"Get out. And stop that sound!" Xyrak barked, and the Shadows quickly obeyed.

Eyeing the urns, Xyrak murmured, "This is the work of Jack Bradford."

In the security corridor, rapid footsteps echoed with the newfound sound of the water droplets. Alysa moved cautiously along the corridor, ducking into a room as six Shadows approached.

The room was a nursery, home to twenty tiny beings protected within the transparent light walls of the angled chamber. Upon spotting Alysa, one small being, Dynam, was startled. Recognizing the intruder, its mouth dropped open in disbelief.

"Hey. Alysa," Dynam stammered, backing away and sprinting towards the open door as if it had seen a ghost. The other little beings watched in silence.

Along a red clearance ledge, Shadows passed by. Suddenly, two hands grabbed the ledge, followed by a head—Jack's head —as he hoisted himself up and silently leaped onto firm ground. He moved cautiously, rounding a bend before Dynam collided with him at full speed. Jack scooped the startled little being off its feet.

"Hey, hold on there, tiger. What's the rush? You look like you've seen a ghost," Jack said just as Alysa appeared.

"She has," Alysa replied.

Dynam looked straight at Jack, eyes wide in disbelief.

"Me?" Jack asked, confused.

"Both of us. No one has *ever* returned from Gyon alive," Alysa informed him.

Dynam backed away and suddenly shouted out, "Anvaky? Anvaky?"

"Shhh, not so loud," Jack warned.

Alysa intervened, "Men, Anvaky." (He's not a robot. He's an alien.)

Perplexed by this orange creature and scared by Alysa, Dynam struggled to break free. "Rys, rys. Sefot," it pleaded.

Jack gently covered Dynam's mouth, sharing a wide smile with Alysa. Her relief at seeing him was apparent, but her tone was urgent. "Jack, we've got to find Sy. Get the crystals back and leave before Xyrak discovers we're here."

"How did you get here?" he asked.

"This is my old neighborhood. Sy?"

"He'll just zap you at the lake again," Jack countered.

"No. Xyrak never does the same thing twice," Alysa replied, her voice filled with conviction.

Dynam growled and tried to bite Jack's hand in an attempt to escape, poking at him all the while.

"They're cute when they're young like this," Jack commented, observing Dynam.

"Jack. Sefot," Alysa reprimanded, her tone conveying more than her words.

Jack was not deterred. "What about her?" he asked, nodding towards Dynam. Alysa looked at him, utterly confused by his line of thought. "We could use her as a decoy. Pretend we're a happy family. You know, mom, dad, and the kid. We'd fit right into this place."

Alysa shot back, "Jack, find Sy."

When he feigned confusion, Alysa began to repeat her instructions, but Jack raised a hand. "Stop. Hey, Alysa. Don't even bother. I've always had this communication problem with women. I'll manage," he assured her before removing his hand from Dynam's mouth.

"You all right, tiger? Are you going to be good now? We may even teach you something," Jack cooed. Dynam accepted Alysa's extended hand, and the two moved away.

"Where are you going?" Jack asked.

"I need some advice. I need some time alone. Meet me at the plaza when you're done," Alysa told him, leaving Jack with the scheming five-year-old.

Jack felt a tug at his suit as he was about to leave. It was Dynam. "How will I know where to find him?" he asked Alysa, who simply responded, "Dynam will show you."

"Hey," Dynam extended a hand to Jack, who took it, stating, "It's your life, kid."

Outside, on Moonstone Way, three friendly colored ghosts were flustered about a singular green pet they had found. Suddenly, a foreign song broke through the echoing plip of the water. Jack and Dynam turned the corner and bumped into the ghosts.

"Hey, how you guys doing? Nice night, huh?" Jack greeted the ghosts. One of them demanded, "Stamyna!"

"Stamina. You bet your little pink suits we got lots of that. Hey, any of you guys see an old man about this high, bald, real smart look in his eye? Name is Sy?" Jack enquired.

Dynam added, "Hey. My name is Dynam."

The Ghosts backed off slightly, clearly unsure about the unusual pair. "Bem. Merym medo?" one of them asked. Dynam shrugged, and the ghosts conferred among themselves.

Jack decided to lighten the mood. "They probably think I'm too old for you."

"Pyntemena. (I'm older than you,)" Dynam retorted, making Jack laugh.

"Merym?" the authoritative ghost finally asked, stepping up to Jack.

"Merym? Merym, merym, merym. Merym on the wall, who's the fairest of them all? Bradford in the morning. Doing a little digging for the big KLOQ. Checking out crime here in Alarym and rumors about folks who cheat at Fyrapo. Seen any?" Jack asked playfully, leaving the Ghosts uncertain.

Looking to solve two problems simultaneously, the Ghosts handed the small green pet to Jack. "Thanks a lot, guys. Don't stand too close together. You might disappear," Jack replied before Dynam was nudged by one of them.

"Fex medo." (Takes three to move, kid,) the ghost told Dynam.

"Takes two to tango, bud," Dynam retorted, and Jack murmured to himself, "Takes two to tango. That's what I was going to say." Then, Jack realized they could read his thoughts, and he theirs. At least sometimes.

17

The city of Alarym was a marvel of architecture, every curve of its structures composed of at least sixty-four polished faces that reflected an array of luminescent beads. The silence of the area was only broken by the occasional dripping water. Jack, Dynam, and their tiny pet companion meandered down Prism Wynd, a street so iridescent and busy it could have been a freeway.

"How are we supposed to find Sy in this place?" Jack grumbled.

Dynam responded simply, "Rystefikya." When Jack looked confused, the child added, "Magic."

"I never said that word. How do you know it?" Jack questioned.

"I learned it from you," Dynam replied with an unsettling amount of certainty. Jack, unsure how to respond, simply retorted, "Let's just find Sy and get out of here."

Behind them, several spectral beings observed their progress with interest.

It was a rule in Alarym that beings traveled in threes. To do otherwise invited suspicion. The open-book nature of the city, its transparent walls, and its lack of individuality unnerved Jack. He glanced back but saw nothing. Nevertheless, they pressed on.

Soon, they reached a vast park, the Crystal Plaza. As they moved through the crowd, they passed a group of Gyonian beings playfully tossing small, colored tetrahedra into a thick blue fluid. Further ahead, they saw a stack of rainbow-hued, paper-thin specters attempting to add dimension to their forms by stacking one atop the other. Dynam tried to nudge one, but it was too rigid to budge.

Suddenly, a middle-aged being moved through the crowd towards them. It held a small white object in its hand and was clearly taken aback by Jack's odd orange appearance. When it stared at Jack, Dynam demanded, "What are you looking at?"

The being replied, "Nothing really." Jack jumped in, "Yeah, what's up here, bud? You want me to join the circus, or you looking for a fat lip from Bradford?" The being backed away, uttering Jack's full name in awe, "Jack Bradford."

Caught off-guard, Jack asked, "How do you know my name?" The being didn't answer. Instead, it called its friends over. They all recognized him, calling out "Bradford" and referencing his popular radio show, KLOQ. Jack was stunned.

Soon, other beings approached, smiling and fingering his bright orange suit. They all held similar small, crystalline objects—Pentyms, they were called—that played Jack's voice. They were listening to his radio show, apparently a hit in this strange city.

Hearing his voice from the Pentyms, Jack felt a shiver run down his spine. He realized the strange dripping sound he had been hearing must have been coming from the transmitter back at the cave. The realization was almost too much to bear.

A proud being stepped up to Jack, holding a Pentym closer

to him. As his voice echoed from the device, Jack turned to see the crowd swelling, a surreal tableau of forms, light, and echoes, their gazes fixed on him.

"Can't fool Bradford in the morning!" a being called out to Jack.

Jack waved off the excited crowd. "Great stuff you guys got here, but I'm looking for someone right now. Not real interested in buying, if you know what I mean."

Observing Jack's uncomfortable demeanor, Dynam asked, "What's wrong, Jack?"

"Think they got copyright clearance on the material, kid?" Jack said as he eyed the crowd.

The crowd parted for them, and just as they were about to move forward, Sy appeared almost out of nowhere.

"Jack, what are you doing?" Sy asked.

"Sy, you old son of a gun. Am I glad to see you," Jack said. "Didn't think you'd made it. Come on. Got to get out of here. This place is driving me crazy."

"You can't leave, Jack," Sy replied.

"Why not? What's wrong?" Jack was growing frustrated.

"Nothing, but you can't leave without knowing what you're doing," Sy advised.

"I know what the hell I'm doing. Just come with me, alright."

"You're being too rash, Jack."

"The hell I am," Jack snapped back.

Sy refused to budge, which increased Jack's frustration. Even as Dynam took Sy's hand in opposition, Jack demanded, "You don't want me to drag you out of here, do you? What's the problem?"

Sy stared at Jack. A deep, knowing look. Then, Jack spotted a group of Shadows approaching the crowd toward them.

"Oh, I get it. Sure, now I see. Divine retribution for the one in the forest, right? You'd think advanced beings would change!" Jack was becoming frantic.

Before they could escape, the Shadows formed a tight circle around Jack, Sy, and Dynam, clearing away the onlookers. "Don't count on it," Jack said defiantly. "I helped Alysa get back here to save you, and this is what I get."

Sy's image broke up and scattered. Jack suddenly realized it was a hologram, a trap to lure him in.

The Shadows, dark indigo beings that appeared to float an inch off the ground, closed in. Jack held up his arms, ready for a fight. When two Shadows looked at each other in confusion, Jack struck one, bending it in half and hurling it at the others.

The fight escalated quickly. A shadow managed to stab Jack with a black crystal, but he fought back, using the crystal to take down his attacker. The crowd watched in stunned silence as the light from the shadow's body faded and died.

A tense silence fell over the park. Jack slowly backed into the crowd, horror and regret etched on his face. "I'm sorry. I'm sorry. I didn't know," he said, dropping the crystal.

In a blink, Jack bolted away, causing the crowd to erupt into chaos. Shadows chased after him, but Jack was running like lightning, his departure leaving a ripple of fear in his wake.

18

Jack darted through streets of crystalline glass, passing startled beings, his panic seemingly mirrored in the infinite corridors and transparent stairwells. He skidded to a halt at a crossroads, gulping for breath and not knowing which way to turn. He made a random choice, anything to keep moving, to give himself time to think.

Meanwhile, rows of Shadows lay plugged into lightboards in Shadow Central, their bodies lit up like beacons. Their glowing feet twitched with pulses of static noise, blips, bleeps, and water-like sounds echoing from their stations. They tracked Jack, their impatience overseen by Xyrak.

Jack finally slowed his frantic pace upon entering the Cerulean Breezeway, a sky-blue-hued pathway bustling with a mix of beings and colored ghosts. Strange pets scampered around, and the beings practically glowed with friendliness toward him like old neighbors whose names they had temporarily forgotten. He played along, immersing himself in the ruse. "Nice dress you've got there, miss. Real knockout," he had said, flashing a charming smile at one of the beings. But as he glanced over his shoulder, they all seemed to drift away, revealing a sight that took his breath away.

The faint but steadily growing sound of water dripping down the corridor ahead resonated. The rhythmic plip, plik, plit echoed from the cavernous end, reverberating through the colonnade and reaching Jack's ears. His eyes were locked on the azure portico at the end, half-expecting the pent-up surge of pulsating blue to burst forth at any moment.

It suddenly struck me like a semi-truck at sixty. I don't know why some things take this long, Jack muttered to himself. *But there was no water in Alarym. No one here needed it except me.*

Parched and sweating, he scanned his surroundings, his thirst intensifying with each heartbeat. *That dripping sound was a primeval reminder to everyone about their roots and the forests of Gyon. About life outside this perfect city, something beyond the game, something even Xyrak couldn't control,* he thought aloud, his voice echoing in the empty street. *But for me, it was a death sentence. If I didn't get out, I wouldn't last. I had to get back to Gyon.*

With a three-day-old beard and a tattered suit, Jack looked like a weary vagabond. He shuffled along the Prism Wynd curb, pulling on a discarded cloak he had found. On the other side of the street, Shadows began their search, moving in and out of the darkened alleys.

A few beings passed by him, their pets in tow. They stole glances his way, whispering amongst themselves. Suddenly, a hooded being waved at him from a doorway. Mystyl, an old master, signaled to him. "Jack, hurry. This way," Mystyl said.

He didn't recognize this ragged being. "Who are you?" he asked, squinting in the dim light.

"Follow me. You'll soon know," was the cryptic reply.

As the Shadows closed in, Jack followed Mystyl, ducking inside an old, decrepit warehouse. They navigated through dusty corridors and up a broken flight of stairs, passing through doors that gave the interior a bombed-out appearance.

As they rounded a corner, Mystyl raised its face to the light, and Jack caught a hint of a smile in the elderly Master's eyes – they were clean, warm, bright, benevolent, and knowing. Mystyl unlocked a door, and they stepped into the unknown.

They went inside Alysa's dwelling, a warm welcome radiating from their host.

"It's okay. These are friends," she assured him, her voice resonating throughout the room, adorned with all the creature comforts suitable for a civilization whose average member barely reached five feet.

Various beings glanced up as they entered, lounging around an open area that overlooked a deep cyan pool. Alysa's gaze fell confidently on her orange-skinned friend, Jack, the focus of all attention.

"They're looking at me a little funny. What do they expect me to do?" Jack asked an edge of concern coloring his words.

"Help them," she responded simply.

"I'm no Superman, you know."

"There's a way of doing things where you do nothing."

"Tell me about it."

"You tell us. You've been doing it all your life. That's how you got here. We saw you fall from the sky. Like Xyrak," Alysa disclosed.

"Look, I know things are a little different here, but that was a mistake. I didn't do it," Jack defended.

"We know. That's why you came. Because you didn't do it."

"What?" Jack blurted out, confusion knitting his brow.

A string of conversations unfolded, revealing they knew where Sy was being kept and how Jack could help retrieve the crystals. They even believed he could fly through walls, something Jack quickly dismissed.

"We know where Xyrak is keeping Sy. Now you can get the crystals," she enlightened him.

"How? Fly through the walls?" Jack's laughter echoed around the room.

"That would work," Alysa responded, not skipping a beat.

Jack looked around the room, his gaze falling on each and every soul - activists, refugees, followers. "Listen, everybody. This is a mistake. I'm not supposed to be here. I don't know how I got here. I don't know how to get back. All I know is that I've got to find that lake on Gyon, or you'll be looking at one very unhappy and dehydrated human being.

"What is dehydrated?" a small voice piped up.

"Beef jerky," Jack responded. Alysa merely nodded, assessing the group.

"Then we're in agreement."

"How? No."

"You believe in Gyon?" she questioned.

"Well yeah, we were there. Remember?"

The beings murmured amongst themselves, impressed. "We will go back with you."

"Fine," Jack stood abruptly, heading for the door. But Mystyl intercepted him, taking his hand and leading him back with a look that held a world of understanding.

"The legend states a strange being from a faraway land would one day come. We would know him as Jack Bradford. The stranger would enter the Dynog. He would know what to do," Mystyl informed him.

"People don't believe in legends anymore. That's a fairy tale. A myth. -- What's a Dynog?" Jack retorted, growing more bewildered by the moment.

Budf appeared from out of the group. Slid up next to Jack. "Well, I see he survived the concentration camps."

"Budf will show you the way," Mystyl promised, prompting Jack to glance at the creature.

"You want me to take him for a walk?" Jack queried, one eyebrow quirked up in surprise.

Mystyl nodded, Alysa, echoing the agreement.

"I can't," Jack protested.

"Why not?" Alysa questioned, looking at him.

"They are looking for me. They'll kill me. That's why."

In response, Mystyl merely shook its head. The other beings rose to their feet, faces filled with strength, renewed hope, and dreams of freedom they could only imagine.

"But I'm not flying through any walls, okay?" Jack reiterated the note of stubborn resistance evident in his voice.

In a lively nursery, a cluster of young beings was engrossed in a heated match of Fyrapo, played on an extensive floor-lit crystal board. They darted back and forth, quick and nimble, moving as rapidly as sparks. The team led by Dynam soon found itself in a dominating position, their strategies eliminating one rival group from the game.

Then, a stalemate befell Dynam. Trapped, the gameboard offered no leeway. Dynam scurried from one end to the other, eyes scanning every angle and possibility only to find no opening. When defeat seemed inevitable, an unexpected hand reached down, presenting the perfect finishing move. In astonished delight, Dynam craned her neck to discover Sy, their old Master.

"Fyrapo," said Sy, a gleam in his eyes.

"Thank you, old Master Sy," replied a grateful Dynam.

The nursery fell into respectful silence, the young beings positioning themselves around the Fyrapo board, their eyes filled with anticipation as Sy prepared to weave a tale.

"Sympfed mytak apom. Ik kelya ryd pintly fel Dynog," Sy began, his voice steady and warm.

The young ones gasped and cooed with excitement. They knew the story. As Sy circled, recreating the tale with his actions, he told them about the wise old Being named Dynog, who once lived in a wonderful palace under the stars, and his great commander Xyrak.

Meanwhile, through a one-way wall, Xyrak observed the group, approving of Sy's captivating narration.

Sy thought he could resist the game forever. Jack's voice echoed. *With stories about life before Fyrapo, about ancestors who lived in Gyon. Now he was losing the game forever.*

Sy, back in the nursery, continued his tale. He told about a time when storytelling was not just a fruitless pastime but a means to link the present with the past. He told of his own exile from Alarym for holding on to this archaic tradition and how Alarym would lose its sole connection to the past with his departure.

Back in Crystal Plaza that night, a horde of beings, engrossed in the pentyms' tales, were disrupted as Shadows stormed the area. Their devices were seized, leaving behind a trail of static. Some of the beings were disillusioned, thinking the stories of Gyon were myths. However, one being held on to his wind mobile, oblivious to the encroaching shadow.

"Fex," the shadow demanded.

The small Being didn't respond.

"Give it up," the shadow insisted.

Turning around, the small being raised a defiant hand, "No pentym, shadow."

Taken aback, the shadow blinked, unable to comprehend this defiance. It was new, it was different, it was confusing.

19

Inside the vibrant nursery, a young being abruptly interrupted Sy's storytelling with an innocent query. "Was there the same magic we have now?" the little one asked.

Sy paused, taking a moment to contemplate his answer. "Magic? Well, I'm coming to that," he began, his eyes glistening with knowledge. "There were many wonderful things out of which came this golden land we call Gyon."

"You mean people went to Gyon?" the young being probed further.

"Oh yes, many times," Sy confirmed.

Just then, Xyrak entered the nursery, a pentym in his hand. With a wry smile, he demonstrated how the sounds of Gyon were nothing but creations of the small white device. "Some believe that little people live inside of here," he remarked, his tone laced with mockery. The young ones erupted into laughter.

"But now we know better," Xyrak added, subtly belittling Sy's narrative. Laughter filled the nursery once again, this time louder and more hearted. Sy was left feeling slighted and humiliated.

.   .   .

Later that night, in the steam-filled Crystal Chamber, Xyrak led Sy in under the escort of Shadows. He looked at Sy with an air of triumph. "Oh, old Master, what a game we've invented. I told you not to come back," he said.

"You caused this," Sy retorted, his voice angry and charged.

Holding up the pentym, Xyrak retorted, "No, it was these. I underestimated their power. Perhaps I underestimated you. The Shadows will collect them until I find the source."

"One day, the people of Alarym will know what you've done," Sy countered, unwavering in his resolve.

Xyrak, however, seemed unbothered. "It won't matter. They have everything they want right now. And the wonderful land of Gyon will remain in our memories as it should, just a myth, a legend, an illusion created by an old Master who defied a Gamesman and lost," he stated, his words slicing through the air.

Moments later, a crystalline cell not more than three feet wide entrapped Sy. A brilliant white light shone over his head, causing him immense pain, as Xyrak and the Shadows left him behind, trapped in the jail cell.

Back in the now-deserted nursery, Alysa and Jack arrived, their steps hushed. Stumbling upon an obstacle, Jack let out a muffled grunt, "Auughh."

"Jack?" Alysa whispered, concern filling her voice.

"Shhh. I know," Jack hushed her, putting a finger to his lips. In their haste, they struggled to unseal a corner door. With their bodies pressed close, Jack couldn't help but succumb to Alysa's warm aura. He stole a swift kiss, immediately pulling back, however. Alysa, taken aback and slightly repulsed, maintained her composure.

"I needed that," he murmured, his voice strained with desperation.

With a deep breath, they resumed their efforts to unseal the corner door.

The Crystal Chamber, aglow with refracting lights like a frozen chem lab in winter, left Jack in awe. Tubes of cadmium orange light and bulbous milori green and blue formations lined the opaque walls and smoke-thin tables.

"Incredible. This place isn't guarded?" Jack asked, glancing at Alysa.

"This is Alarym," she replied, her tone making it clear that the explanation was unnecessary. She sealed the door behind them, ensuring their solitude.

"Alysa, why didn't we come here before?" Jack queried, his curiosity still piqued.

"We needed new crystals," she said, her tone simple and matter-of-fact.

"In every third cycle of Fyrapo, new crystals are made. We had to wait." She shushed Jack with a finger to her lips, turning her attention to the soft cobalt mist that floated through the room.

Alysa and Jack discovered a cache of lackluster crystals in another part of the chamber. After a careful examination, Alysa passed one to Jack. He mimicked her actions, inspecting the crystal with an inexpert eye.

Drawn by curiosity, Jack found himself exploring an anteroom. It resembled a futuristic oven with various colorful symbols reflected on a small panel. Nestled below, a tiny, luminous figurine, ball-shaped, sat next to a crystal.

"New Gyonians. They're born here in the cycle of Fyrapo. It

goes on forever. Life and death in your words," Alysa explained, her face alight with what Jack could only describe as maternal pride.

As they observed, a rotation of color pulsed through the panel, causing the small ball to glow more intensely. A connection clicked in Jack's head — the glowing orb, the glow within the beings themselves, the magic crystals — it was all interconnected.

His examination was cut short, however, by a shocking discovery. Sy — defeated, suspended, and barely conscious was encased in a crystalline cell on the rotating panel. The pentym lay smashed at his feet.

Alysa tried to unseal the cell with her crystal in a flurry of desperate action, but each attempt failed. She raced back for more crystals while Jack reached out to touch the cell wall. Sy, in a final act of connection, raised his hand to the wall against Jack's before collapsing. A nearby dark blue crystal faded to black, reflecting the grim situation.

Alysa returned, her reaction minimal. She shared a look with Jack before whispering, "No."

In the depth of the night, Jack led Alysa out of the Crystal Chamber. Suddenly, her control shattered, and she screamed, throwing the crystals and violently smashing every one in the mist-filled room.

"No!" she cried, her voice echoing through the chamber.

20

In Shadow Central, a solitary shadow observed an irregularity in its light sequence. It interacted with a red light that subsequently turned blue. Pressing another, it returned red — all was well. The puzzled shadow activated another bank of signals, uncovering a spinning red alarm that raced around the screen's perimeter. A grid sweep confirmed an unsettling truth: the Crystal Chamber had been breached.

Hitting the alarm, the shadow set the unit aglow with blue. The state of emergency it represented was an alien, chilling signal that reverberated throughout the complex.

Meanwhile, Jack and Alysa, casually strolling through a conduit with a few concealed crystals, were interrupted by the alarming sound echoing through the tube. The beings, pets, and ghostly figures around them scattered, seeking shelter in available units.

"Let's get out of here," Jack urged, breaking into a run with Alysa close behind.

Outside, in the Cerulean Breezeway, the alarm's echoes

meshed with the soft, make-believe winds. Beings and colored ghosts scattered as a rogue Lighter Than Air Crystal Carrier (LAC) sailed through the breezeway, crashing and trapping a small, thin, yellow-orange pet beneath its golden glow. The LAC looked like a super advanced open-cockpit spaceship. Six Shadows descended from it, filing into every third door.

In the Crystal Chamber, Xyrak, flanked by two escorts, arrived at a devastated scene. Unhappy, he scanned the shards of shattered, melting, and deforming crystals starting to form inside the thick walls. To him, it looked like a plague in need of eradication.

Simultaneously, a Chief shadow orchestrated a frantic search at Prism Wynd Through-pass, a narrow intersection on a three-dimensional grid. "Find them. Check up there. The rest down here!" He barked orders as units of Shadows were dispatched to various light quadrants.

Above them, a mix of air traffic filled the sky, each LAC suspended in its own light frequency corridor. Big ships, small ships, fast ones, and slow ones. Their crossing paths created brief flashes of day within the night, sparking like trolleys in midair as they overlapped in their trajectories. Below, the alarm and discord continued.

Further, along Moonstone Way, a trio of Shadows raced along, peering into every third home's glass-like surface as they passed.

Finally, three Shadows broke into Alysa's unit, agile and quick. Their search was fruitless, finding only the silence of an empty room.

In the Carrier Bay, a semi-circular ledge extended into the openness of Alarym. The floor was illuminated with a deep, royal blue hue. Docked with geometric precision, six crystal carriers rested. A patrol of three Shadows boarded one unlit Lighter Than Air Crystal Carrier (LAC), igniting its lights before revolving slowly and taking off. As they did, another LAC corkscrewed into a vacant slip, its six Shadows dismounting and heading for the exit as its lights faded.

Peeking around the open bay doors, Jack observed the scene, Alysa standing guard. He darted through the darkness to the nearest LAC and settled into the pilot's seat. His fingers depressed invisible buttons on the armrests, yet nothing happened. A lone shadow, returning to the bay, spotted him and began to approach. Jack tried to remain calm, pressing the armrests again. A small surge of color fluttered inside the LAC, and a slight whirring sound hinted at some form of response.

"Stamyna!" the shadow called as he approached Jack. Yet, the carrier remained stubbornly still. The shadow touched Jack, asking, "What do you think you're doing?"

"Nothing," Jack replied nonchalantly, slamming his fist on the panel and kicking the side of the carrier in frustration. "Needs gas," he added, storming off.

Jack regrouped with Alysa, the confusion evident in his voice. "Now what?"

"Jack, if you'd gone to the Dynog first..." Alysa began.

"Well, I didn't go to the Dynog first. You said we needed Sy for that, and in order to get Sy, we needed those crystals. Look, do you want to stay here, or do you want to go?" Jack shot back. Their gaze shifted to the shadow inside the carrier bay, who was clearly using some kind of communications device.

"Do I have a choice?" Alysa asked a tone of resignation in her voice.

"This isn't Bloomies, baby," Jack retorted. By the time the shadow looked back, they were gone.

Alysa and Jack dashed along the glowing, translucent ledge

of the Red Clearance. Jack found the strut he had used earlier and started crawling across to the portal, Alysa following a few feet behind.

Meanwhile, Jack lay flat on his stomach high above the Crystal Plaza, catching his breath in the dark. Suddenly, three LACs appeared out of nowhere, weaving in formation along the red ledge, making figure eights of light around the strut. Surrounded, with no possible escape, Jack was instructed to stay put. Resigned to his capture, he surrendered himself onto the deck of one of the LACs. Statuesque Shadows encircled him as the pilot maneuvered the carrier into a steep dive into the upper reaches of Alarym, with the other two carriers following in perfect formation. Alysa, safely hidden in the shadows, looked on in despair.

Later, in a Goldenrod Conduit, Jack was led briskly up through a spiral corridor in military formation, three Shadows in front and three Shadows behind.

His voice echoed in his mind: *Alarym was a city without waste. Everything had a place. Everyone served a function. No one was ever left out or left alone. They belonged to each other. And it worked! The game kept the city going. -- That is until I showed up. A walking heresy to Fyrapo. A one-man time bomb in a china shop. I didn't fit in.*

21

―――――

A door opened in the heart of the vast, triangular Operations Center, allowing Jack to enter. Alone in the enormous space, he ambled around, gazing in awe at the sweeping view of the city below him. Patches of dark and light glowed rapidly in various shimmering areas, their streams of color reflecting off a wide assortment of darkly colored panels, all arranged in a unique variety of geometric shapes.

From afar, he noticed a small group of Vienna Green Ghosts making way for an entering Master in a purple-tinted chamber. Their flat green sides gave them the appearance of cardboard Christmas trees. Jack felt a pang of sadness.

Without warning, a dull thud echoed through the chamber. Jack spun on his heel, coming face to face with Xyrak. The figure stood proud, regal, serene, a curiosity in this place.

"If you're not Gyonian, nor are you a robot, then what are you?" Xyrak questioned, his gaze piercing Jack.

"If we asked you that question, what would you say?" Jack retorted, refusing to be intimidated.

"Answer the question," Xyrak persisted.

"I am your biggest nightmare. But then again, this might only be a dream," Jack replied, his tone playful despite the situation.

Xyrak moved to a small tabletop unit, touching a light pod. The room filled with the sound of dripping water. Jack smiled, shrugging, "You need a plumber."

"Yes," Xyrak responded, his understanding of English almost immediate. His intelligence was unsettling to Jack. After turning the sound off, Xyrak proclaimed, "Quiet now."

"Serene," Jack responded.

Xyrak nodded, dismissing Jack gracefully. The Shadows escorted him out as Xyrak glanced over the complex.

In the Silver Tetrahedra, an inverted and highly reflective holding cell, Jack found himself suddenly gripped by an intense headache. A Fyrapo board sat in the center of the cell with Dynam and Budf, the two-dimensional dog pet, positioned along the edges of the triangular configuration.

When Xyrak looked at me, it felt like a clamp on my brain. I was sure he could read my thoughts. That means he would know everything, and there was nothing I could do, Jack reflected.

"Ohm on the raynge, Jack," Dynam beckoned.

"Hardly," Jack retorted.

"Play with us," Dynam invited, placing a colored piece on the board. Budf followed suit, surprising Jack. He reluctantly sat down and played along, but his focus waned as he felt outmatched by Dynam and even Budf.

Once all spaces on the board were occupied except the center triangle, the game reversed. Jack found himself losing, unable to make a solid move.

"Fyrapo," Dynam declared.

"Beaten by a short kid and a show-off mutt. What is this place, a kennel or a nursery?" Jack spat, standing up to pace the cell.

Three Shadows entered, their gaze fixated on Jack.

"Let's go," one of them ordered.

"Where?" Jack asked.

"You'll see when we get there," the shadow replied cryptically.

"If I don't come back, you can take my turn," Jack quipped at Dynam and Budf, who were still engrossed in their game. He slapped a shadow on the back and led the way out without another word.

A sudden, explosive flash of white light faded, revealing Xyrak standing chest-deep in a fluid-filled underwater cavern. A droplet of water fell on his forehead, prompting him to wipe it off. His broad hand reached for the transmitter, causing the VU meter to flutter slightly.

"Fyrapo!" Xyrak stated, seizing the small black unit before flashing out of the cavern.

In the Dynog Narthex, the world around Jack was predominantly triangular, its wall white from apex to base, save for a tiny mouse hole-like black semi-circle along the center baseline. An ear-piercing shrill echoed in the small chamber, followed by a flash of light. The angled sides of the room closed in, abruptly halted, and the sound vanished. The once-white wall was swallowed by darkness, from which Xyrak emerged, Jack's transmitter in hand.

The door to the Crystal Chamber swung open, and Shadows ushered Jack inside through the swirling mist. A sudden, potent nausea overcame him, causing him to crumple in discomfort.

"Aauughh," Jack groaned.

"What is it?" a shadow asked.

"Food poisoning," Jack grimaced, staggering to the wall. "I need a doctor."

The shadow gestured towards a cell reminiscent of the one Sy had been held in, "In there. The pain will stop."

Jack spun into a roundhouse kick, summoning his remaining strength, forcing the shadow back into the waiting cell. "Get your silly ass in there, white boy!" he grunted, hitting the wall switch, trapping the shadow inside. "And don't stay in too long. You'll get sunburned."

He turned to find himself surrounded by nine large Shadows. "Oh shit," Jack muttered, diving into the steam-filled room and losing himself in the misty chaos.

The door flung open in the nursery as Jack burst in, disrupting the ongoing storytelling. As the Shadows chased him, he vaulted over one little being after another, aiming for a high strut that led to an open balcony. He swung over the brace, crashing through the glass door and hanging from a bar above the balcony.

"Next time, I'll try the handle," Jack muttered, assessing the five or six-story drop below him. As Shadows advanced towards him, one stepped on his hands, prompting him to threaten, "Get off me, pal, or I'll blow your transistors."

Rummaging through his pocket, Jack found a pen and jammed it into the shadow's under-sole, causing it to spark. A lighter-than-air crystal carrier sped past, and Jack waved, "Taxi!"

Ignoring him, the carrier moved on. However, another carrier slowed its rotation, and Mystyl, Alysa, and a ghost pilot emerged from the light cone.

"Jack, hurry. Get on," Alysa beckoned.

"No, I'm waiting for somebody," Jack replied hesitantly.

"Get on," Alysa insisted.

"Can I jump through that light?" Jack asked, uncertain.

"Don't you trust me?" Alysa responded.

Jack eyed the spinning carrier nervously, the risk of falling to his death weighing heavily on his mind. "You sure?" he asked.

"Jump," Alysa commanded.

As Shadows seized his arms and legs, Jack bit at them to break free, then took a leap of faith onto the safety of the LAC. The pilot pulled away, and the craft corkscrewed into the night.

22

The sweeping city surrounded them, glowing against the backdrop of darkness as they sped through the skies in the LAC.

"Xyrak got the transmitter," Alysa announced.

"I know." Jack queried, the sense of uncertainty hanging in his voice.

"The water sound stopped," Alysa replied, her words causing a prickling sensation of apprehension in Jack's mind.

"It's just the pentyms," Jack tried to brush it off, seeking comfort in denial.

"No. It's over, Jack," Alysa corrected him, her words hitting him like a punch to the gut.

"You mean he took me off the air? He can't do that," Jack protested, the full impact of Alysa's words slowly settling in.

The LAC swirled to a halt at Umber Close, and Jack, Alysa, and Budf disembarked. Alysa assured them she would signal when they were done. Mystyl reached out, taking Jack's and Alysa's hands in hers one last time.

"Krosda," Mystyl said solemnly before the LAC powered up and spun away into the vast cityscape.

"Follow Budf, Jack. I'll wait here," Alysa instructed.

Budf led the way, darting along a mid-brown passage before abruptly halting at the final turn. Jack caught up, panting slightly.

"What is it, Budf?" Jack asked, looking around warily.

Ahead of them was a catwalk, a light bridge connecting the Dynog Narthex's entrance to the brown, V-shaped security corridor. Guarding the tunnel entrance were three Shadows.

"In there?" Jack queried, feeling a knot of dread tighten in his stomach. As if understanding Jack's apprehension, Budf suddenly took off.

"Hey, Budf, back here, boy," Jack called after the pet, his heart pounding.

Just as Budf neared the shadow guard post, Alysa managed to distract the trio, their attention redirected to the other half of the close. With the Shadows off guard, the passage momentarily clear, Alysa gave Jack a knowing glance and followed the Shadows out.

Outside, on the Diatonic Lightbridge, Jack found himself on a fifty-foot, acromatic run. It was like a smoked glass tube that extended horizontally over parts of Alarym. Suspended only at its source, the other end of the passage hung mid-air. Behind Jack and Budf, the two brown tunnels took on a V-shape as three more Shadows made their way to guard the catwalk entrance.

Footfalls echoed ominously behind Jack, the sound growing louder, more threatening. Looking ahead, the light bridge seemed to rise slightly. Budf sprinted ahead over the rise while the floor beneath Jack seemed strangely familiar. He was standing on a patchwork of red wires cross-patched with large blue bulbs, which constituted the under-surface of the floor.

The sound of the Shadows' pursuit spurred Jack on. He

moved quickly, but an unseen force seemed to propel him forward. His walk turned into an uncontrollable run. Jack was racing ahead like walking on hot coals, his feet barely touching the ground.

A quick glance down revealed the red wires and blue bulbs transforming into a churning mass of unreleased energy, surging upwards and forcing him onward. Before he knew it, the light bridge ended abruptly, ejecting him into a mid-air dive.

As he plummeted down into the twilight, there was no land below, only pathways of crystal and towering glass structures. The star-filled night twinkled falsely as he fell, holding back a scream, getting what he'd asked for in the first place.

He sped downward, hurtling toward a series of structures. It felt like he was about to crash. Then, the city walls suddenly unfolded, reflecting various bright colors before transitioning into a blinding white light.

Jack landed, miraculously in one piece, inside the mysterious inner sanctum, the Dynog Narthex. A white and triangular space except for a small black mousehole along the floor. Budf, his loyal companion, quickly gave Jack a comforting lick before scampering through the mousehole.

"Budf. Wait," Jack called out to the disappearing figure of his pet. However, where the walls had previously moved for Xyrak, nothing stirred for Jack. With desperation, Jack crouched down on his hands and knees. Covered in dust and grime, he forced his bulky frame through the dark carbon hole with the grace and ease of a caged-in rat.

Emerging on the other side, Jack found himself deposited amid four-and-a-half-foot-high needles of light that filled a precise rectangular space, floating and rotating in a dark void. His hand reached for one of the light needles to pull himself up, but it shattered upon contact. A shard of the broken glass struck Budf, who let out a pained cry before vanishing.

"Budf?" Jack called out, panic seeping into his voice.

"No longer here," a soft voice echoed all around him, and it took Jack a moment to realize it was his own.

"Who are you? What happened to him?" Jack demanded, casting his gaze around to locate the source of his voice.

Above him, a vaulted ceiling displayed a moving panorama of moonlight and stars, stretching out to infinity and creating the illusion that he was standing atop a mountain.

"Another move. Arrangement," the voice that sounded like Jack's echoed.

"Whose arrangement?" Jack asked his question echoing in the mysterious chamber.

"Not important," came his own voice, the eerie response hanging in the air.

"Who are you? Why's that my voice?" Jack pursued, his tone firm and insistent. His queries, however, were met with a heavy silence.

"This is ridiculous," he finally vented, aghast at the unsettling echo of his voice. The disembodied responses seemed to anticipate his thoughts before they were even fully formed.

"Answer the question yourself," his voice insisted from the ether. Jack shivered. The sensation of his thoughts being read proved unnerving.

He attempted to regain some semblance of control. "Okay, tell me. How did I get here? Wait. Don't tell me. I know. It's not important."

"Not important," the voice echoed back, its mimicking tone grating on his nerves.

His irritation sparked more inquiries. "Why were those three out in Gyon? Alysa, Sy, Hym?"

"Removed from Fyrapo," came the cryptic response.

"What did they do?"

"Resisted Fyrapo."

"But Xyrak took Sy back?" Jack probed further, trying to make sense of the unfolding mystery.

"New game," the voice cryptically supplied.

"So, if I resist, I get a new game?"

The chamber lapsed into a seemingly thoughtful silence before Jack, alarmed, quickly added, "Cancel that. Wait. A new game didn't get Sy anywhere. How do I win this one?"

"Fyrapo everywhere. Everything."

"I've noticed that, but how do I know if I'm doing the right thing, playing the right game?"

"Not important." The whisper came.

The dismissive response gnawed at Jack. "If this thing is everywhere, but it's not important, then what is?"

His question seemed to resonate within the chamber, the ensuing pause feeling especially charged. The dimly lit needles surrounding him appeared to collectively hold their breath.

"Krosda," his voice finally breathed out, sending a shiver down his spine.

"That's what Alysa and Mystyl keep telling me. What does that really mean?"

"Trust."

"Intuition?"

"Not that simple."

"This is crazy. This is my own voice talking to me. -- Why am I here?"

"To help, Jack."

"Help who?"

"Help Jack."

"Me? I've been stumbling through this place for days. How do I help myself now?"

"Help others."

Jack paused, battling his mounting confusion. "If you know everything, there's something I need answered. My wife?"

"Beth." The voice said.

"She was just turning..."

"Thirty-one."

"When it happened. The accident."

"The intersection. Second and H Streets."

His words hung heavy in the air, his distress palpable. "How can you know? How?"

The chamber provided no response, leaving Jack to relive his loss in painful silence.

"Your daughter," his voice broke the quiet.

"Tell me something. Why did they have to die like that?" he asked, desperation creeping into his voice.

Again, the silence was tangible.

"Not important."

"If that's not important, then what the hell is? What the hell means anything? You son of a bitch. What the hell are we here for?" Jack exploded, pacing frenetically, his teeth gritted in rage.

In his fury, he smashed a light needle with his fist, the sharp pain doing little to quell his torment. He collected his thoughts, calming himself momentarily.

"This is crazy. I'm talking to myself. Why did they have to die? Why now? Why like that?"

Again, his questions were met with an unsettling silence. Regaining composure, Jack paced the room, trying to pull himself together.

"Alive, Jack. Never dead. Always one more move. Fyrapo," his voice echoed, leaving Jack stunned.

The chamber was suddenly filled with the blare of a car horn, the screech of tires, and the chilling sound of a collision, followed by police sirens. The sounds were all too familiar. The last thing he needed to hear.

"Beth?" Jack's voice was a whisper, his heart pounding as he breathed deeply in the dark chamber.

The room transformed around him as if he were traveling in a bucket of light through a bottomless space. His hand found another needle, which began to glow under his touch.

"Beth?" he called out again, his voice barely more than a broken whisper.

23

An alarm emitted a weak signal in this part of town, akin to an air raid siren on a rainy night. Small creatures tossed tiny tetrahedra into the rushing sewer fluid. Mystyl dropped Jack and Alysa off, promising to return in five minutes before disappearing again. The pair swiftly melded into the crowd.

A discreet Chief Shadow and his two accomplices navigated through the anxious masses, their eyes scanning the surroundings. Jack and Alysa continued their dance, slipping in and out of clusters of people and keeping away from the patrolling shadows.

"What did you find out?" Alysa asked, her eyes never leaving their surroundings.

"It's okay. We can go. We should see who else wants to leave," Jack responded, leading her through the crowd.

"What do you want me to do?"

"Stick together for once."

Ignoring her perplexed look, Jack scaled up to the luminous top of the fountain. The spindly metal struts around him fluttered and glowed, casting strange shadows on the ground below.

"What are you doing?" Alysa called from below.

"When they take away the radio, and they shut down the press, this is all we've got left," he shouted back down at her, sweeping an arm out to encompass the bustling crowd. "The speaker's corner like in Hyde Park in London."

Alysa furrowed her brow, then scaled the structure herself. "What?" she asked, now standing next to Jack.

"The town square. This is the way we do it where I come from. You want some attention. I'll get you attention. You want to get saved. I'll get you saved," Jack explained, looking down at the sea of faces below them.

"Stop this!" Alysa hissed, glancing anxiously at the approaching Shadows.

"You think we can hide in your crystal world and play our way out of this one. No. Xyrak's not going to just let us walk out of here. He wants to put us on ice. Understand?" Jack ignored her, instead raising his voice to address the crowd. He created quite the stir, and it took the Shadows a moment to react.

He began to rally the beings, inviting them to join him in his flight from the city.

"Hey, who's ready to get out of this stinking place, huh? Who wants to go fishing, mountain climbing, play some golf?" Jack's voice rang out into the space, filled with confidence and a daring that seemed misplaced.

His proclamation was met with stunned silence. The crowd of beings just stared at him, their faces a mask of bewildered confusion.

Alysa rolled her eyes and pretended not to know him, but some of the beings looked intrigued. Jack's shout pierced the heavy silence, provoking an immediate reaction from the beings. It took a moment for the Shadows to react, their dark forms stiffening in surprise.

The beings began whispering among themselves, and a couple climbed up the fountain monument to join Jack and Alysa. The Shadows closed in, but Jack continued his passionate speech, injecting the crowd with hope and rebellion.

From his side, Alysa clamped a hand over his mouth, her voice carrying a warning tone.

"Jack, no."

Undeterred, Jack continued, pulling Alysa's hand away from his mouth. "Don't worry. I've pulled bigger stunts than this in college."

Their audience, the Shadows, started to close in. "Great," Alysa said sarcastically.

"That's what we need, folks. Great men, great women, and great children. Why? Because there's life out there on Gyon. We all know it. Right? So who's kidding who? We've been there. And we're going back. So who wants to sign up?" Jack's voice carried over the crowd, his energy infecting the silence.

Alysa seemed nervous, making a show of pretending not to know him again.

"I feel like Paul Revere. You know what I mean?" Jack turned to Alysa, but she gave him a blank look, clearly not understanding his comparison.

A couple of beings glanced at each other, their faces confused. "What is he saying about Gyon?" one of them asked.

"Return to Gyon," replied the other.

"Return there? It doesn't exist." The first being was doubtful, but the other simply nodded.

Sensing the rising tension, the Shadows started to press through the crowd and began to climb the monument after Jack.

"Look, even these guys want to go. That's right. We'll all go. Faxod Gyon," Jack called out, prompting Alysa to correct him.

"Fex Gyon."

"Thanks. We'll fex Gyon and fix this place too. New rules by Jack Bradford. What do you say?"

The Shadows closed in, just a few feet away now, and beings started to follow them up the monument. Faces from the crowd began to emerge, faces they had seen before.

"Alysa is going back now," one being declared.

"To a place that doesn't exist?" questioned another.

"Sounds good to me," a third being chimed in, followed by an echo of agreement.

Jack and Alysa circled away as the Shadows neared, climbing higher up the monument. The Shadows followed, but their light feet couldn't grip the slippery surface. They slipped and stumbled, but their determination was unwavering.

The crowd below was alive now, charged and electric. The thought of returning to Gyon hung heavy, sparking excitement and fear. Sensing danger, some beings and colored ghosts attempted to leave the scene, trying to avoid getting involved. Others threw tiny crystals at Jack, who smiled at Alysa as a crystal whizzed past his head.

"It's nice to know you're loved," he joked, ducking as another crystal flew past him.

Meanwhile, a chant, "Gyon," began to echo through the crowd, their voices gaining momentum as more beings joined in. Jack and Alysa climbed even higher up the monument. Shadows and beings scrambled all over the spiny wet structure as it swayed and moved in the wind.

When it seemed like the Shadows had cornered Jack, a LAC carrier performed a rollover and swooped in beside them. The rotation slowed, revealing Mystyl at the helm, accompanied by Dynam. Jack and Alysa scrambled aboard the ship with other beings, and together, they lifted off, leaving the monument and the chanting crowd behind.

"Gyon, Gyon, Gyon!"

. . .

Mystyl piloted the craft with the skill of an expert, the ship an almost invisible shaft of light in the night. Jack glanced back at the swirling, surging stream of colors illuminating the panels in the streets below. Spotting a pickup, Alysa gestured for Mystyl to guide the carrier down.

Below, Shadows rounded up rebellious beings in a military-like fashion, invading their living spaces and placing Masters with strange creature pets. It was a restructuring that was anything but equitable or fair, as orders from Xyrak blared from speakers, inciting panic on the streets.

Mystyl's carrier swooped down, and beings of all kinds rushed towards it, clinging to its bottom or scrambling to get on. Jack lent a hand to those struggling to get on, urging them to hurry, even as Shadows attempted to yank them off. Some made it; some didn't.

As Shadows reached to pull down the craft, Mystyl hit a light panel, flushing the carrier into a roll and lifting off. Jack managed to help one last being into the vessel before Mystyl took them into the night, the craft racing into overdrive.

Inside the carrier, Jack surveyed the diverse beings they'd picked up. Their dark eyes were wide with fear, their small bodies fragile and scared. Some understood what was happening, others looked lost and confused. Jack placed a firm, reassuring hand on one being's shoulder. "You're going to be all right. You understand? You and your family are going to be all right."

Arriving at the upper mountain wall, the carrier hovered near the broken portal Jack had first entered. Six other carriers arrived simultaneously, each piloted by a being whose radiance matched Mystyl's. Together, the small armada provided a luminous platform for the beings to escape one by one through the portal. Jack helped those who struggled, urging them to climb.

Suddenly, a squadron of carriers flew into their airspace, piloted by Shadows. Alysa was the first to notice, whispering in the frosty air.

"Shadows," Alysa warned, her eyes locked onto the emerging squadron of carriers flying towards them from below.

"I know. You ready?" Jack retorted, a grim determination settling on his face as he braced himself for the impending ascent through the portal. Their escape plan, however, took a jarring turn as Mystyl unexpectedly sent the carrier plummeting down a hundred feet in a matter of seconds, fingers deftly pressing a sequence of red buttons.

The dramatic drop worked. They all successfully made it through the portal, their carriers instantly speeding towards another exit higher up. Before long, only Jack, Alysa, Dynam, and Mystyl remained a squadron of carriers getting closer, their presence increasingly imposing.

"Jack, come on," Alysa urged, her voice straining with effort.

"Trust yourself, Jack, or you'll never reach Gyon," Mystyl interjected, her tone stern. Jack was caught between making his own ascent or aiding Dynam.

Without warning, Mystyl left him no room for choice. Jack grappled in the open space, his heart pounding with adrenaline. Alysa, witnessing his struggle, extended an arm towards him, her grip precarious but determined. As high-speed crafts intercepted their path, the night was bathed in a dazzling spray of light, casting surreal shadows around them.

Jack's fingers, slick with cold sweat, slipped on the icy ledge of the portal. His breath hitched. Alysa stretched an arm to help him, her grip barely strong enough to assist. High-speed craft intercepted them, turning night into day with a spray of light. With desperation, Jack mustered every ounce of strength within him. With a final, determined pull, Jack hauled himself up to safety, escaping the imminent threat of the approaching carriers.

The refugees found themselves in a frozen, steaming tunnel thick with emerald-green patches of foaming smoke. Through this, a line of beings fled the complex, their clothes ill-suited for the cold. Jack returned to help the stragglers, urging them to keep moving, get their blood flowing, and assist each other.

"Come on, keep moving. Just go. Hey, you back there. Get up. Swing your arms. Get the blood flowing. Pick it up back there."

The beings marched on. Tired, ragged, and freezing. Despite their exhaustion and the freezing cold, the beings marched on, Jack amongst them, pressing his hand against the ice wall and sucking on an icicle to quench his parched throat.

"Come on. Keep it up. You're gonna freeze if you don't move. Help that man up. -- Alright."

He encouraged them to keep going, avoid freezing, and help each other. This was their new reality, for now.

24

Within the underbelly of the mountain, the seemingly unending passages stretched on.

Finally, it broke open, and the ragged troop looked out, facing an icy lake in the distance. It looked like the wind-swept barren landscape of Antarctica. Jack broke away from Alysa to assist those struggling at the back of their band of refugees.

"Grab my hand," he urged, but his words met confusion.

"What do you mean?" one of the beings questioned.

"Take it," Jack responded with urgency. The beings followed his lead and moved quicker with Jack's help.

"Hey, everybody, hold hands like this. Hold on to each other," Jack instructed, then took off to ensure everyone understood his command. Upon rejoining Alysa, a shared smile was their unspoken conversation.

"You're doing just great. Keep it up. Just keep moving. You got it?" Jack's encouragement seemed to help, and Alysa responded with an appreciative smile. A rugged, mountainous pass was before them high above the lake. The trail was treacherous.

The sound of crinkling ice teased their ears; the exit was not far off.

The night revealed a network of glowing caverns, from which flowed a procession of beings, spectral forms, and pets, all shivering in the cold. They edged along the icy cliffs, assaulted by snow flurries. Occasionally, a being lost its footing and plummeted to a chilling death below. Jack turned to Alysa.

"How are you doing?" he asked.

"It's difficult through here." She responded, her voice almost drowned by the howling blizzard.

"We'll make it through," Jack affirmed.

The reluctance to continue grew among the fifty survivors as they arrived at the water's edge on the planet's dark side. The lake seemed passable, but there were icy flows they needed to navigate, and they did not have a boat. The situation looked grim. Two older beings began to bicker, blaming each other for their predicament.

"Hey guys, knock it off. We have to stick together, you understand? No one is going back now," Jack interjected, but his words fell on deaf ears as the disgruntled beings began to trudge back.

Jack caught up to the oldest being. "What are you doing? You can't go back. You don't belong there," he warned.

"I can."

"And what do you suppose you'll do once you're back inside, huh?" Jack challenged.

"Stay there forever," came the resigned response.

"Anyone else? Now is the time," Jack called to the remaining group, his gaze fixed on the floating ice in front of them. No one moved. "Alright. That's settled. Now I want everyone to find a piece of ice big enough to stand on and keep moving. Just jump, like this, from one to the other. If someone falls in, we pull him out. Got that?"

The beings looked at him blankly, and Jack turned to Alysa.

"You know what to tell them." He jumped onto a block of ice and started the treacherous crossing.

Soon, all the refugees were hopping between floating ice fragments. Panic erupted as several beings fell into the frigid water. The others, never having seen water before, didn't understand the danger.

A young being approached Jack when a more prominent being's leap destabilized its ice raft. The youngster plunged into the freezing depths. Jack saw this and dropped into the water after the child. Two other beings also fell in and latched onto Jack in panic, dragging him under.

"Swim. Pull yourself up. Krosda. Krosda," Jack managed to babble through mouthfuls of icy water.

With great effort, he hauled all three beings back onto the ice. Alysa watched silently as Jack saved the shivering beings from the icy abyss.

The darkness of the glacial night embraced the group, but Jack, soaked and freezing, ignored the biting cold and pushed on.

"Come on. We keep moving. No giving up. Not now. Not ever," he urged.

Battered by the elements, the troop reached the far shore and pressed through the snowy fields. High-speed winds shrieked around them, and the weaker members of their party fell behind, struggling to push through the mounting snow drifts.

"No one said it would be easy," Jack stated grimly.

"We keep going?" Alysa asked, her voice barely audible over the gusts of wind.

"Yeah, and no one gets left behind," Jack affirmed.

"We keep going, Jack. Good," Alysa echoed his determination.

Suddenly, Jack's voice echoed through the mountains. "We all go, or no one goes. You got that?"

Undeterred by the biting cold, Jack went back for those struggling. "No!" His cry startled the beings, reverberating off the frozen walls of the mountain. He helped the dying to their feet, providing just the encouragement they needed to continue. The gratitude in their eyes spoke volumes, and Alysa, watching this display, began to understand.

Forced into action, Alysa also began to help, lifting the weary to their feet and steering them through the relentless storm. Jack's smile of appreciation warmed her more than any fire could.

Suddenly, a fleet of crystal carriers descended upon the group. Hooded beings, some mere spectral outlines, piloted the craft. The pilots hovered just above the ground, taking on the weakest members of their party.

"Where's Mystyl and Dynam?" Jack asked, worry creasing his brows.

"Mystyl, Dynam. Are you there?" Alysa called out, but her query was met with confused glances from the spectral beings and other members of their party.

Undeterred, Alysa continued to help others board the carriers, setting an example for the rest to follow. The scene was a chaotic blend of chilling winds, flashing crystal carriers, swirling blizzards, dark robes, shadow and light, and the imminent threat of an approaching tempest.

Arriving at the canyon's summit, Jack and Alysa looked over the landscape.

"Look, there it is," Jack said, pointing toward the distant deep forest.

"Gyon," Alysa echoed, a sense of belonging filling her. The sight of the lush forest brought smiles to the faces of their beleaguered group. Alysa placed her arm around Jack's waist.

"We made it," she murmured.

"We're home. This is your home," Jack affirmed. The storm abated.

From above, the twin moons of Gyon emerged, performing a dazzling dance for their weary spectators. However, one light seemed to break away, diving straight at them. It soon became apparent that it was a LAC. Onboard, Jack spotted Dynam and two friendly Pink Ghosts.

"Hey, Dynam," Jack greeted, relief washing over him as the little being jumped from the craft and ran toward him.

"Home on the range, Jack," Dynam replied, and Jack couldn't help but laugh, lifting the little being onto his shoulders.

"That's right, Dynam. Home on the range," Jack affirmed.

"Where's Mystyl?" Alysa asked.

"Alarym is Mystyl's home," Dynam responded solemnly.

As their survivors began to descend the steep canyon, the pools below reflecting the last rays of the moonlight, Jack spotted an unsettling sight through the smoky mist.

At the edge of the forest, two long bands of color stood out, one white and one black. The white hovered over the black. Jack squinted, his heart sinking as he identified the white line as a stream of two hundred crystal light carriers. The dark shadows beneath them began to part, revealing the ominous figure, Xyrak.

"No. It can't be," Jack whispered, horror creeping into his voice. He stared at the battle formation, his heart heavy. "Not now. Why?" he murmured, the question lost in the wind.

25

———

The timid beings, trembling in the biting cold, huddled around Jack. Their faces a mirror of apprehension and terror. Alysa broke the silence, her voice trembling.

"What are we going to do?"

Silence hung heavy in the air, punctuated by the soft gust of the wind.

"Jack?" Alysa pleaded again.

Jack's face hardened. "It's a trap. We've walked right into his trap."

The dread that hung in the air seemed to thicken. Alysa's voice was barely a whisper. "Now what?"

Ignoring the looks of fear, Jack started to descend alone. Alysa and Dynam, their hands clutching each other, tried to stop him.

"No, you stay here. Both of you." He said. "He doesn't want you. It's me he's playing against. That's what it's about. It's between him and me," Jack explained, his voice barely audible against the wind.

Alysa's gaze bore into Jack, her eyes brimming with tears.

Suddenly, Dynam and Alysa threw their arms around Jack, holding on tightly to this odd, orange-bearded creature they'd considered a friend.

"No, you can't. Silly human. When will I see you again?" Alysa's voice was choked with emotion.

Jack pulled back, giving them both a small smile. "Just remember. No regrets."

Alysa's words echoed in the chilling wind, their secret good-bye. "Meta fel maxsik hey Alysa. (In this world, they call me Alysa.)"

"That's what you said when we met. Hello, goodbye," Jack's voice was soft, the words lingering in the air before being swept away by the biting wind.

"Don't do it, Jack," Alysa pleaded again. But Jack was already walking away, giving Dynam a last, lingering hug.

"See ya later, kid. Keep up those flying lessons," Jack's voice was cheerful, but his eyes told a different story.

Dynam and Alysa stepped after him, but Jack was resolute. He gave Alysa one final hug, his eyes telling her all the words he couldn't say.

"You can't destroy a legend," He declared before descending the steep slope.

Separated by the expanse of a blood-red pool. The atmosphere charged, their silence heavy as the crimson mist swirled around them in a macabre dance. Crimson steam from the blood-red pool seemed to whisper accusations as Jack and Xyrak faced off. The wind carried their words away, leaving the simmering tension in the air.

"Well, what do you want to do?" Jack broke the silence, his voice steady despite the impending threat. "Blow each other's brains out or discuss it like intelligent intergalactic beings?"

Xyrak responded with a grand sweep of his arm.

"Fyrapo," Xyrak challenged.

A brilliant white flash sliced through the atmosphere, shattering the tense calm. A high-speed hiss followed, dissipating into the obscurity of the storm. The heated, red mist that had hovered over the pool's surface was abruptly frozen mid-air, its form contorting and crinkling into shards of ice. These icy fragments rained onto the pool's surface, puncturing the water and disturbing its stillness. The impact created a unique pattern of ripples that expanded and collided with the edge before finally dissolving, leaving behind a trail of freezing crystals.

Transported in a flash, Jack and Xyrak stood on different magnificent peaks, facing off against each other in the blizzard. The electric tension in the air was palpable, lighting up the dark sky with platinum streaks. The wind howled and screamed, carrying with it bursts of ice and snow.

Xyrak zapped to Jack and knocked him off his feet. A ferocious battle ensued between them, man against the alien, their bodies moving like blurs against the icy backdrop. Brutal punches were thrown, dirty tactics used, and in the end, they both fell, tumbling down into a bottomless crevice. The falling crystal sparkled between them, their last lifeline in the violent storm.

They were prepared for the worst, a 10,000-foot drop, their bodies bracing against the unending fall, the world around them fading into a soft pastel of orange and white. Jack and Xyrak disappeared, leaving behind the volatile landscape echoing the raging sounds of the storm, desperate voices reduced to mere echoes in the chaotic cacophony.

26

On earth, the shrill ambulance siren cut through the quiet day, an orange blur of activity swarming around Jack. He was sprawled on the ground, grappling with his own body. Blood smeared his face, and pain contorted his features, but his eyes were alive, defiant.

From Jack's perspective, the world was a dizzying whirl of colors and shapes, indistinct voices merging with the siren's wailing. A damp hand was placed over his eyes, blocking the chaotic scene. Voices whispered around him, growing in intensity before being drowned out by a deafening rumble.

"Pel my whyt apeen deh, Jeeek. See zem thane. How ny thane," the producer's voice filtered through the noise, an alien melody in the dissonance.

"Yey fed gatimtu uhysp tytal," responded a paramedic, his words fading into the background as another wave of pain hit Jack.

"Xy -- rak," Jack managed to grunt out between gasps of pain.

"Whyt? Dygu hairwhyt deezit?" The producer seemed startled by Jack's words, her voice rising in surprise.

"Hessdel ryus. Prop bayleynt rynel bleykyng tu," the paramedic continued, oblivious to the producer's shock.

A small boy, eyes wide and fearful, stared at the commotion. He glanced between Jack, the producer, and the paramedic before his gaze landed on the top of the tent on the airfield. No hole. The red lights of the ambulance illuminated his innocent face before the paramedics loaded Jack in, and it sped away.

As the ambulance departed, Jack's world filled with a mix of sounds; the siren's frantic pulse, the crowd's murmur, and the hum of traffic. An oxygen mask was strapped to his face. His breath was shaky against the cool plastic. But a smile tugged at the corners of his mouth as he looked out at the sky, the familiar blue bringing a sense of peace.

"Things will be alright, Jack. Trust me. Please trust me," the producer's voice was quivering and concerned.

Jack attempted to respond, but his words were lost, his consciousness fading. As he drifted unconscious, the producer reached into his pocket, her fingers brushing against something hard. She pulled out a glowing crystal, its ethereal alien beauty mesmerizing.

As the ambulance sped through the city streets to the hospital, it was quickly swallowed up by the early morning traffic.

Days Later

Jack was sitting in bed inside the hospital room, his face clean and without any injuries. His eyes, once filled with pain, now held a calm warmth. The nurse busied herself around him, fluffing his pillow and pouring him a glass of water. He took the glass, his gaze fixated on the clear liquid.

"Feeling better?" she asked, her voice kind.

"Much," Jack replied, his voice more robust than before.

The nurse gave him a warm smile. "Doctor says you can go home tomorrow."

Jack's gaze lingered on the window, the blue sky a welcoming sight. "I am home," he replied, a soft smile on his lips.

27

———

S now pelted the exterior of a rundown motel, the flakes accumulating to reach the windowsills. Most rooms were dark, but one glowed against the harsh winter night.

Inside that room, a biting gust whipped at the tattered valance, ushering in a dusting of snow that settled onto a pile of newspapers. The room was lit by a feeble yellow bulb, illuminating the cracked ceramic fixtures. Jack poured himself a glass of Perrier, his eyes darting over a manuscript of typed pages amidst the clatter of fervent typing by an unseen occupant.

Later, in a bustling upscale restaurant, his producer nursed a Bloody Mary while she waited for Jack's belated arrival. A waiter lingered nearby, ready to take his order.

"Something to drink, sir?" the waiter asked as Jack settled into his seat.

"Perrier, a twist of lime, please," Jack replied.

"Six months ago, you were a confirmed Scotch drinker," his producer observed, a smirk tugging at the corners of her mouth.

"I'm an aquaholic now," Jack retorted with a chuckle.

"Well? You've kept me in suspense." The producer leaned in, eager for Jack's revelation.

He handed her a packaged manuscript and said, "You want the story? Here's the real story." The title read: *SHADOW RUN, My Adventures Abroad* by Jack Bradford. "I felt you deserved the first copy."

"Thank you." The producer seemed taken aback. "And I have something for you."

She retrieved the radiant crystal from her purse and placed it on the table. It was as stunning as ever, a piece of the Dynog chamber. Jack was stunned. "Where did you get this?"

"It was in your jumpsuit," she revealed.

"You've had it all this time?" he asked, stunned.

"I've been meaning to return it, but I just never got around to it," she confessed. Jack could hardly contain his excitement. He was happy, elated. He held up the crystal.

"Do you realize what this means?"

"Man disappears for three minutes. Ages five days. Where did he go?" the producer questioned.

"Now I have proof," Jack declared triumphantly, mesmerized.

"Proof?" she asked.

"Alien artifact. Read."

The producer turned to the final page of the manuscript, her eyes scanning over the words that Jack had been weaving throughout their narrative.

The irony was I never knew who won," Jack's voice seemed to echo from the parchment. *"Xyrak could have captured them. Returned them to Alarym, or maybe he just let them go. For a brief instant, our two cultures had crossed. They didn't believe in me, and we didn't believe in them until now.*

He examined the crystal again while the producer continued reading aloud.

"Like so many things in life, it was an unknown. Like love, death, like losing everything you've got. That's what happened to them. No one to help them, no one to trust, drifting through time for the rest of their lives in a land I could never forget."

On Gyon

The scene shifted within the manuscript's words. An early light warmed Shadow Run, where a gathering of beings, ghosts, and pets huddled in a circle, their heads bowed in quiet reverence. Alysa their leader.

"Thy kingdom come, Thy will be done on earth and everywhere as it is in heaven," she murmured.

Dynam and Alysa stood solemnly before two handmade crosses marking the ground while the others congregated for the strange burial chant.

"For thine is the kingdom and the power..." Alysa's voice trailed off, allowing Dynam to pick up the thread.

"...and the glory. Amen. It's all I could remember," they said together, their voices harmonizing with shared grief.

They fell silent, standing in respect for a long moment before Alysa finally spoke again. "Plant a cross. Say a prayer," she instructed.

One by one, the group members shared their cryptic parting words.

"Can't fool Bradford in the morning," one stated.

"Who knows the way to earth?" a second being asked.

A third whispered, "Get those wipers on and watch out for oil on the freeway."

When it was Alysa's turn, she gently lifted Dynam, singing softly.

"Oh, give me a home where the buffalo roam and the deer and antelope play."

Others joined in the odd chorale, their voices rising and falling with the melody. "Where seldom is heard a discouraging word and the skies are not cloudy all day.

The group disbanded and headed over to a flotilla of LAC crystal carriers. Nearly all the beings climbed aboard. However, Dynam and Alysa walked hand-in-hand down the canyon toward the forest.

Fully loaded, the carriers arced up and swiveled over in a display of glowing lights against the twilight. They glided past the vibrant steaming pools, a second glitter illuminating their recharge in midair before they soared over the first range of hills toward the lakes.

As they walked, Alysa began another song, smiling at Dynam as they chimed in with the lyrics, their voices blending harmoniously with the evening.

"This land is your land. This land is my land. From Alarym to the New Lake Island. From the Gyon forest to the Shadow waters."

Above them, twin moons broke through the dense maroon clouds, casting two brilliant paths of light for Alysa and Dynam to follow.

"This land was made for you and me," they sang together, their voices fading into the night.

"How often at night when the heavens are bright
  With the light from the glittering stars
  Have I stood here amazed and asked as I gazed
  If their glory exceeds that of ours."
- My Western Home, Dr. Brewster M. Higley VI, 1871

REVIEW

If you liked this book, please fee free to leave an honest review.
Thanks so much.

http://www.amazon.com/review/create-review?&asin=
BoCDNTNHB5

ALSO BY A.C. JETT

- A Warm Winter Chill
- <u>Abduction</u>
- The Albatross
- The Architect
- Bad Brakes
- Calabasas Hills
- Crash Site
- Desperado
- Earthlight
- Fast Track
- <u>Final Appeal</u>
- Gideon's Fault
- Hal, The Spud King
- Healing Time
- Heartstorm
- High School
- Hypocrisy
- Identity
- Nefarious
- One More Time
- Powder Stream
- Red Ink on Steel
- Sense of Duty
- Shadow Run
- Special Feature Live!
- Stage Fright
- Star Children
- Wanderlust
- Warm Body

HEALING TIME

In an alien star field, a space station circled a ragged planet enveloped by thick clouds. At the same time, two distant moons spun in opposing trajectories.

Far from Earth, a colony grappled with a lethal plague. Until a cure was found, the Intergalactic Council had quarantined the afflicted planet.

The survivors were holed up in a bunker, attempting to piece their lives together amidst the ruins of their society. Every individual had dual roles in this desperate fight for survival. Doctors donned battle gear, businessmen stood guard, and scientists labored over cooking pots. A fierce wind battered the shelter from the outside, its howl echoing through the bunker.

A group of survivors huddled around a large table, the haunting strains of Mahler echoing from a tape recorder.

"Hey, shut that door. It's infecting my soup," a thick-set man grumbled, placing his dirty boot on the table for emphasis.

"You're eating slop, and you don't even know what's in it," an ugly guy retorted.

"I know what's not in it," the thick-set man quipped as a man in a white coat, a chef, ladled out more gruel.

"Pass," said the ugly guy.

A tough woman polished her flamethrower.

"You got to do that at the table?" the ugly guy asked.

"You know a better place?" she replied without skipping a beat.

Immersed in Emerson's writings, an Italian man ignored the underlying tension that seemed to grip the crowded bunker. Eight guards returned from their shift complaining about missing meals and laid their weapons aside.

"You're up, the guard stated.

"I haven't even had dessert," said the thick guy.

"Yeah? I haven't had breakfast," said another. He and the tough woman strapped on their exotic gear.

"I'm telling you, man, this place is running over with stinking drones. I can smell them real close," a Black guard warned his compatriots.

"Hey, Johnson, It's probably your socks," A thin guard retorted with a jab at his hygiene.

"I saw a scout team. They was mean and ugly muthers," Johnson insisted, sniffing at the tough woman's neck.

"That was no scout team, Johnson. That was your dick," she shot back, fastening her laser launcher with precision.

Amidst this back-and-forth, children were busy inspecting and dividing bread rolls, ensuring everyone got a share. With deep blue eyes, a young girl California bore the brunt of the shortage with stoic acceptance while her neighbor feasted on crumbs. California's mother, Arizona Teal, washing stacks of dishes, noticed her daughter's empty plate. "Here, honey." She took a candy bar from her pocket and gave it to California, whose eyes sparkled with joy.

"Thanks, Mom," California said.

"It's the last one we have," Arizona warned.

The tough woman looked at her handling food. "What, no gloves, Teal?"

She showed off her rubber gloves, riddled with holes. "We've all been exposed."

Wearing dirty white protective gear, several men returned from an outside trip. One of them, Andrew, removed his headgear and kissed Arizona on the neck. The couple's deep connection was palpable as Arizona's arm instinctively wrapped around him. Andrew hugged his daughter, California, and expressed relief at returning safely.

"So glad you made it back," Teal said.

"Barely," he confessed, replying to Arizona's relieved statement. "You get enough to eat?" he asked his daughter.

"I was at the end of the line," California responded.

"You'll get your turn tomorrow," he reassured her.

"Did you find something?" Arizona Teal asked.

"A few signals. We're pretty sure that's it," Andrew responded, leaving an air of uncertainty hanging over the bunker.

In the depths of the night, within a room lit by the glow of table maps, Andrew, Teal, and Cal huddled together. Their hands clasped in a tender yet urgent embrace as they scrutinized the large elevation map of the alien landscape. It was a web of blue lines indicating vast land loss and restructuring.

"Low-frequency inbound repeaters in this area. Pretty weak. But this has got to be it," Andrew asserted, his voice filled with a weary optimism.

Another figure detached himself from the shadows, shedding his white protective gear. Ed Fullbrite, an older, greying man, exuded an air of scholarly wisdom. He was a comforting reminder of the civilization they all yearned for.

"Man-made, Teal. God knows how it shifted more than eighteen degrees, but it's the only one on this planet," Fullbrite added, his voice steady and sure.

"I can't believe it," Teal murmured, her voice a blend of awe and disbelief.

"If we're right, this should lead us to the serum lab," Fullbrite confirmed.

Elsewhere, a radio operator monitored multiple channels at the communications console. The room hummed with the ambient chatter of radio transmissions and intermittent static.

"Clocking twenty-two oh two on three niner. Mountain Mole, confirm at Echo," he transmitted, his voice crisply professional.

"Echo in. All silent here," came the voice over the radio, shortly followed by another, "Delta, ditto. We're locked up for the night."

Back at the map table, Fullbrite pressed a button, summoning his staff. "Let's pack. We've got a long journey ahead of us," he said, his tone conveying urgency and resolve.

"Ed, if we let Michael help, we could manage this sooner," Andrew suggested, hinting at a buried familial bond.

"You're too trusting of your brother," Teal countered, her voice laced with wariness.

"I think he would help us now," Andrew defended. "We're all in this together."

"Honey, it didn't work before. What makes you think he has changed?" Teal countered, her skepticism clear. Andrew's hopeful glimmer seemed to diminish at her words.

Amid a tempest outside, a single radio stood against the wind's fury, sand and rain driving relentlessly.

Inside at the communications console, the radio operator tried to clear the static from the storm. "This is Mountain Mole on three one. Come in, Romeo. Do you read?" His query met with a hiss and a vague grunt that might've been a voice. The radio operator's smile bloomed, albeit briefly.

"Romeo say again. -- Appears we have mag interference. If you are unable to respond, confirm status ten, sir, and click twice," he instructed, maintaining his calm demeanor.

A hand, desperate and trembling, clawed through the muck for the microphone. It was abruptly halted by a heavy boot.

A steel blade glinted ominously in the dim light, flashing red against a bare throat before the owner's lifeblood seeped into the muck below. A dirty hand basked in the blood, letting it pool in his palm and fingers. A distorted figure, a heavily armed mutant drone, lifted the blood-soaked hand to its mouth, savoring the warm, coppery taste.

"Romeo, this is Mountain Mole. Please click your mic if you confirm, sir," the radio operator's voice echoed hauntingly from the abandoned radio.

In response, the drone leisurely licked his bloody hand, then slowly reached for the microphone. He clicked the switch twice.

The radio operator registered the double click at the console inside the bunker. "Roger Romeo, advise if the problem persists," he said, unaware of the gruesome reality behind the response.

Healing Time